The voices from the ranch house took on a note of urgency.

She guessed that the marshals had discovered Jack's escape. The arm he'd wrapped around her tightened protectively. If she relaxed and allowed her body to melt into his, she knew she'd be overwhelmed.

More than once, she'd asked herself why she was so invested in Jack's rescue. The big reason was utterly apparent. He was a good man, trying to do the right thing, and he didn't deserve to be threatened, especially not by the men who were assigned to protect him.

And it didn't hurt that he was hot. Being close to him set off a fiery chemistry that was anything but high-minded. She didn't want to lose him.

ABOUT THE AUTHOR

Though born in Chicago and raised in L.A., Cassie Miles has lived in Colorado long enough to be considered a semi-native. The first home she owned was a log cabin in the mountains overlooking Elk Creek, with a thirty-mile commute to her work at the *Denver Post*.

After raising two daughters and cooking tons of macaroni and cheese for her family, Cassie is trying to be more adventurous in her culinary efforts. Seviche, anyone? She's discovered that almost anything tastes better with wine. When she's not plotting Harlequin Intrigue books, Cassie likes to hang out at the Denver Botanical Gardens near her high-rise home.

Books by Cassie Miles

HARLEQUIN INTRIGUE

904—UNDERCOVER COLORADO †
910—MURDER ON THE MOUNTAIN †
948—FOOTPRINTS IN THE SNOW
978—PROTECTIVE CONFINEMENT*
984—COMPROMISED SECURITY*
999—NAVAJO ECHOES
1025—CHRISTMAS COVER-UP
1048—MYSTERIOUS MILLIONAIRE
1074—IN THE MANOR WITH THE MILLIONAIRE
1102—CHRISTMAS CRIME IN COLORADO
1126—CRIMINALLY HANDSOME
1165—COLORADO ABDUCTION**
1171—BODYGUARD UNDER THE MISTLETOE**
1177—SECLUDED WITH THE COWBOY**
1193—INDESTRUCTIBLE
1223—LOCK, STOCK AND SECRET BABY ††
1229—HOOK, LINE AND SHOTGUN BRIDE ††
1255—MOUNTAIN MIDWIFE
1279—UNFORGETTABLE

†Rocky Mountain Safe House
*Safe House: Mesa Verde
**Christmas at the Carlisles'
††Special Delivery Babies

CAST OF CHARACTERS

Caitlyn Morris—She remembers too much. After years as an embedded reporter in the Middle East, she retires to the family cabin in the mountains to heal.

Jack Dalton—A protected witness at a mountain safe house, he escapes the men who want to kill him, but he has amnesia. Is he Greg Perez, a hitman? Or Nicolas Racine?

Heather Laurence—Owner of the Circle L Ranch, this rangy cowgirl is an old friend of Caitlyn's.

Danny Laurence—Heather's brother, a local heartthrob, is now married and a deputy sheriff.

Mark Santoro—Jack remembers him as a murdered friend and the head of a crime family based in Chicago.

Gregorio Rojas—Using the alias Mark Reynolds, Greg heads a drug cartel and wants Jack dead.

Tom Rojas—The older brother of Greg will be convicted of murder if Jack testifies.

Drew Kelso—One of Greg's bodyguards, he's a killer.

Bob Woodley—A local congressman and retired schoolteacher, this elderly gent is one of Caitlyn's mentors.

Steven Patterson—The U.S. marshal nearing retirement betrays his duty.

Ned Bryant—The young Texan marshal has learned all the wrong lessons from Patterson.

Hank Perry—The third marshal at the WitSec house.

Chapter One

Morning sunlight sliced into the rocky alcove where he had taken shelter. A blinding glare hit his eyes. The sun was a laser pointed directly into his face. He sank back into the shadows.

If he stayed here, they'd find him. He had to move, to run…to keep running. This wasn't the time for a nap. He shoved himself off the ground where he'd been sleeping and crouched while he got his bearings.

Behind him, the rock wall curved like bent fingers. Another boulder lay before him like a giant thumb. He had spent the night curled up inside this granite fist.

How did I get here?

Craning his neck, he peered over the edge of the thumb. His hideout was halfway up a slope. Around him were shrubs, lodgepole pines, more boulders and leafy green aspen trees. Through the trunks, he saw the opposite wall of a steep, rocky canyon.

Where the hell am I?

His head throbbed. The steady, pulsating pain synchronized with the beating of his heart.

When he raised his hand to his forehead, he saw a smear of dried blood on the sleeve of his plaid, flannel shirt. *My blood?* Other rusty blotches spattered the front of his shirt. *Was I shot?* He took a physical inventory. Apart from the killer headache, he didn't seem to be badly hurt. There were scrapes and bruises but nothing serious.

By his feet, he saw a handgun. A SIG Sauer P-226. He checked the magazine. Four bullets left. *This isn't my gun.* He preferred a Beretta M9, but the SIG would do just fine.

He felt in his pockets for an ammunition clip and found nothing. No wallet. No cell phone. Not a useful packet of aspirin. Nothing. He wasn't wearing a belt or a holster. Though he had on socks, the laces of his steel-toed boots weren't tied. *Must have dressed in a hurry.*

He licked his parched lips. The inside of his mouth tasted like he'd been chewing on a penny. The coppery taste was a symptom, but he didn't know what it meant. *I could ask the paramedics. Oh, wait. Nobody's here. Nobody's coming to help me.*

He was on his own.

His fingers gingerly explored his scalp until he found the source of his pain. When he poked at the knot on the back of his head, his hand came away bloody. Head wounds tended to bleed a lot, but how had that blood gotten on the front of his shirt?

He remembered shots being fired in the night. A fist-fight. Running. Riding. On a horse? *That can't be right.* He wasn't a cowboy. Or was he?

No time for speculating. He had to move fast. In four days…

His mind blanked. There was nothing inside his head but a big, fat zero.

In four days, something big was going down, something life-changing and important. Why the hell couldn't he re-member? What was wrong with him?

The chirp of a bird screeched in his hypersensitive ears, and he was tempted to go back to sleep. If he waited, the truth would catch up to him. It always did. Can't escape the truth. Can't hide from reality.

He closed his eyes against the sun and gathered his strength. A different memory flashed. He wasn't in a forest but on a city street. He heard traffic noise and the rumble of an overhead train. Tall buildings with starkly lit windows loomed against the night sky. He fell on the pavement. Shadows devoured him. He fought for breath. If he lost consciousness, he would die.

His eyelids snapped open. Was he dead? That was as plausible an explanation as any.

This mountain landscape was the afterlife. Through the treetops, he saw a sky of ethereal blue. One thing was for damn sure. If he was dead, he needed to find an angel to tell him what came next.

CAITLYN MORRIS STEPPED onto the wide porch of her cabin and sipped coffee from her U.S. Marine Corps skull-and-crossbones mug. A crisp breeze rustled across the open meadow that stretched to the forested slopes. Looking to the south, she saw distant peaks, still snowcapped in early June.

A lock of straight blond hair blew across her forehead. She probably ought to do something about her messy pony-tail. Heather was going to be here any minute, and Caitlyn didn't want to look like she was falling apart.

She leaned her elbows on the porch railing and sighed. She'd moved to the mountains looking for peace and solitude, but this had been a busy little morning.

At daybreak, she'd been awakened by an intruder—a dappled gray mare that stood outside her bedroom window, nickering and snorting, demanding attention. The mare hadn't been wearing a bridle or saddle, but she had seemed tame. Without hesitation, she'd followed Caitlyn to the barn. There, Caitlyn kept the other two horses she was renting for the summer from the Circle L Ranch, which was about eight miles down the winding dirt road that led to Pinedale.

After she'd tended to the wayward horse, sleep had been out of the question. She'd gotten dressed, had breakfast, put in a call to the Circle L and went back to the horse barn to check the inventory slip for the supplies that had been delivered from the hardware store yesterday.

A handyman was supposed to be starting work for her today, even though it was Saturday. Most of her projects didn't require two people, but she needed help to patch the barn roof. She checked her wristwatch. It was almost nine o'clock, and the guy who answered her ad had promised to be here by eight. Had he gotten lost? She really hoped he wasn't going to flake out on her.

When she saw a black truck coming down the road, her spirits lifted. Then she noticed the Circle L logo and the horse trailer. This wasn't her handyman.

The truck pulled into her drive and a tall, rangy brunette—Heather Laurence, half-owner of the Circle L—climbed out. "Good to see you, Caitlyn. How are you doing?"

There was a note of caution in the other woman's voice. Nobody from this area knew exactly why Caitlyn had come to live at this isolated cabin, which had been a vacation home for her family since she was a little girl with blond pigtails and freckles.

She hadn't wanted to tell her story, and folks from around here—even someone like Heather, whom she considered a friend—didn't push for explanations. They had a genuine respect for privacy.

Caitlyn held up her skull-and-crossbones mug. "Would you like some coffee?"

"Don't mind if I do."

The heels of Heather's cowboy boots clunked on the planks of the porch as they entered the cabin through the screen door.

When Caitlyn arrived here a month ago, it had taken a week to get the cabin clean enough to suit her. She'd scrubbed and dusted and repainted the walls of the front room a soothing sage green. Then she'd hired horses for company. Both were beauties—one palomino and the other roan. Every day since, she'd made a point of riding one in the morning and the other in the afternoon. Though she certainly didn't need two horses, she hadn't wanted to separate one from the others at the Circle L. No need for a horse to be as lonely as she was.

Sunshine through the kitchen windows shone on the clean-but-battered countertops and appliances. If she decided to stay here on a more permanent basis, she would resurface the counters with Turkish tile.

"Looks nice and homey in here," Heather said.

"It had been neglected." When she and her brother were living at home, the family spent every Christmas vacation and at least a month in the summer at the cabin. "After Mom and Dad moved to Arizona, they stopped coming here as often."

"How are they doing?"

"Good. They're both retired but busy." Caitlyn poured coffee into a plain blue mug. "Cream or sugar?"

"I take it plain and strong." Heather grinned. "Like my men."

"I seem to remember a summer a long time ago when you were in love with Brad Pitt."

"So were you."

"That sneaky Angelina stole him away from us."

Heather raised her coffee mug. "To Brad."

"And all the other good men who got away."

They were both single and in their early thirties. Caitlyn's unmarried status was a strategic career decision. She couldn't ask a husband to wait while she pursued her work as a reporter embedded with troops in war zones around the globe.

"That crush on the gorgeous Mr. Pitt must have been fifteen years ago," Heather said. "A simpler time."

Fifteen years ago, September eleventh was just another day. Nobody had heard of Osama bin Laden or the Taliban. "Before the Gulf War. Before Afghanistan."

"You've been to those places."

"And it doesn't look like I'll be going back any time soon." A knot tightened in her throat. Though Caitlyn wasn't ready to spill her guts, it wouldn't hurt to tell her old friend about some of the issues that had been bothering her. "The field office where I was working in the Middle East was closed down due to budget cuts."

"Sorry to hear it. What does that mean for you?"

"I've got a serious case of unemployment." And a lot of traumatic memories. Innumerable horrors she wanted to forget. "I'm not sure I want to continue as a journalist. That was one of the reasons I came here. I'm taking a break from news. No newspaper. No TV. And I haven't turned on my laptop in days."

"Hard to believe. You were always a news junkie, even when we were teenagers."

"Your brother used to call me Little Miss Know-It-All." Her brother was four years older and as cute as Brad Pitt. "I had such a huge crush on him."

"You and everybody else." Heather shook her head. "When Danny finally got married, you could hear hearts breaking all across the county."

Danny was still handsome, especially in his uniform. "Hard to believe he's a deputy sheriff."

"Not really. Remember how he always played cops and robbers?"

"Playing cowboy on a ranch is kind of redundant."

After days of solitude, Caitlyn enjoyed their small talk. At the same time, she felt an edge of anxiety. If she got too comfortable, she might let her guard down, might start welling up with tears, might turn angry. There was so much she had to hold back.

She looked through her kitchen window. "Do you know a guy named Jack Dalton?"

"I don't think so. Why?"

"He answered my ad for a handyman. And he was supposed to be here over an hour ago."

"Caitlyn, if you need help, I'd be happy to send over one of the hands from the ranch."

She wanted to remain independent. "This guy sounded like he'd be perfect. On the phone, he said he had experience as a carpenter, and he's a Gulf War veteran. I'd like to hire a vet."

"You spent a lot of time with the troops."

"And I don't want to talk about it. I don't mean to be rude, but I just can't." Suddenly flustered, she set down her mug on the countertop. "Let's go take a look at the horse that showed up on my doorstep."

After years of being glib and turning in daily reports of horrendous atrocities, she hated to find herself tongue-tied. Somehow, she had to get her life back.

WEAVING THROUGH THE BOTTOM of the canyon was a rushing creek. He sank to his knees beside it and lowered his head to drink. Ice-cold water splashed against his lips and into his mouth. It tasted good.

No doubt there were all kinds of harmful bacteria in this unfiltered water, but he didn't care. The need for hydration overwhelmed other concerns. He splattered the cold liquid into his face. Took off his flannel shirt and washed his hands and arms. His white T-shirt had only a few spots of dried blood.

As far as he could figure, he'd been sleeping in his boxers and undershirt. He'd been startled awake, grabbed his flannel shirt and jeans, jammed his feet into his boots and then…

His scenario was based on logic instead of memory. The remembering part of his brain must have been damaged by the head wound. His mind was like a blackboard that had been partially erased. Faint chalk scribbles taunted him. The more he concentrated, the more they faded. All he knew for sure was that somebody was trying to kill him.

This wasn't the first time he'd been on the run, but he didn't know why. Was he an innocent victim or an escaped felon? He suspected the latter. If he'd ever rated a guardian angel, that heavenly creature was off duty.

His first need was for transportation. Once he'd gotten away from this place, he could figure out what to do and where to go.

He tied the arms of his flannel shirt around his hips, tucked the SIG into the waistband of his jeans and started hiking on a path beside the creek. Though it would have been easier to walk along the nearby two-lane gravel road, his instincts warned him to avoid contact.

The canyon widened into an uncultivated open field of weeds, wildflowers and sagebrush. This landscape had to be the Rocky Mountains. He'd come to the Rockies as a kid, remembered hiking with a compass that pointed due north. It was a happier time.

A black truck hauling a horse trailer rumbled along the

road. He ducked behind a shrub and watched as the truck passed. The logo on the driver's side door read: Circle L Ranch, Pinedale, Colorado.

Good. He had a location. Pinedale. Wherever that was.

He trudged at the edge of the field near the trees. His head still throbbed but he disregarded the pain. No time for self-pity. He only had four days until…

He approached a three-rail corral fence in need of repair. Some of the wood rails had fallen. Two horses stood near a small barn which was also kind of dilapidated. The log cabin appeared to be in good shape, though.

He focused on the dark green SUV parked between the cabin and the horse barn. That would be his way out.

A woman with blond hair in a high ponytail came out of the barn. Around her waist, she wore a tool belt that looked too heavy for her slender frame. At the porch, she paused to take a drink from a water bottle. Her head tilted back. The slender column of her throat was pure feminine loveliness. That image dissolved when she wiped her mouth on the sleeve of her denim shirt.

He didn't want to steal her SUV. But he needed transportation.

Coming around the far end of the corral, he approached.

When she spotted him, she waved and called out, "Hi there. You must be Jack Dalton."

It was as good a name as any. "I must be."

Chapter Two

Caitlyn watched her new handyman as he came closer. Tall, lean, probably in his midthirties. He wasn't limping, but his legs dragged as though he was wading through deep water. Rough around the edges, he hadn't shaved or combed his thick, black hair. His white T-shirt was dirty, and he had a plaid shirt tied around the waistband of his jeans.

When he leaned against the corral fence, he seemed to need the rail for support. Was he drunk? Before ten o'clock in the morning? She hadn't asked for references. All she knew about Jack Dalton was that he was a veteran who needed a job.

"On the phone," she said, "you mentioned that you were in the army."

"Tenth Mountain Division out of Fort Drum, New York."

Colorado natives, like Caitlyn, took pride in the 10th Mountain Division. Founded during World War II, the original division was made up of elite skiers and mountain climbers who trained near Aspen. "Where were you stationed?"

"I'd rather not talk about it."

After the time she'd spent embedded with the troops, she had a great deal of empathy for what they had experienced. To be completely honest, she had self-diagnosed her

There were plenty of lies he could tell her about why he was armed, but an efficient liar knows better than to volunteer information. "It never hurts to be prepared."

She gave a quick nod, accepting his response.

Apparently, he was good at deception. When she'd asked about his military service, he hadn't hesitated to cite the 10th Mountain Division, even though he didn't remember being in the army or being deployed.

His story about the car accident had been a simple and obvious lie. Everybody had car trouble. Claiming an accident prompted automatic sympathy.

If he'd planned to stick around for more than a couple more minutes, he would have felt bad about lying to her. She was a good woman. Kindhearted. When he'd said he was hurt, she'd rushed to help him, offered her shoulder for support.

Taking his gun with her, she headed toward the kitchen. "I hope egg salad is okay."

"Yes, ma'am."

"I told you before, call me Caitlyn. I'm not old enough to be a ma'am."

And you can call me Jack, even though I'm pretty sure that's not who I am. He rolled the name around in his memory. Jack Dalton. Jack. Dalton. Though the syllables didn't resonate, he didn't mind the way they sounded. Henceforth, he would be Jack Dalton.

Caitlyn poked her head into the dining room. "If you want to wash up, the bathroom is the first door on the right when you go through the living room."

He followed her directions, pausing to peek into the closet near the front door. If he was going to be on the run for any period of time, he'd need a jacket. A quick glance showed a couple of parkas and windbreakers. Nothing that appeared to be his size. A rifle stood in the corner next to the vacuum cleaner.

At the bathroom, he hesitated before closing the door. If the men who were chasing him showed up, he didn't want to be trapped in this small room with the claw-footed tub and the freestanding sink. He checked his reflection in the mirror, noting the bruises on the right side of his face and a dark swelling on his jaw. Looked like he'd been in a bar fight. Was that the truth? Just a bar fight? The simplest answer was usually the correct one, but not this time. His problems ran deeper than a brawl. There were people who wanted him dead.

He searched the medicine cabinet. There was a wide selection of medical supplies. Apparently, a woman who swaggered around with a tool belt slung around her hips injured herself on a regular basis. He found a bottle of extra-strength pain reliever and took three.

After trekking through the forest, his white T-shirt was smeared with dirt, and he didn't exactly smell like a bouquet of lilacs. He peeled off the shirt and looked in the mirror again. In addition to patches of black and blue on his upper right arm and rib cage, a faded scar slashed across his chest from his clavicle to his belly button. He had a couple of minor scratches with dried blood. A deeper wound—newly healed—marked his abdomen. *What the hell happened to me?* These scars should have been a road map to unlock his memory.

Still, his mind was blank.

He washed his chest and pits. His worst injury was on the back of his head, but there wasn't much he could do about it. No matter how he turned, he couldn't see the damage.

There was a sound outside the bathroom door. A car approaching? They could be coming, could be getting closer.

Damn it, he didn't have time to mess around with bandages or sandwiches. He needed to get the hell away from here.

He slipped through the bathroom and looked out the front window. The scene in front of her house was unchanged. Nobody was coming. Not yet.

Caitlyn called out, "Hey, Jack."

"I'll be right there."

She charged into the living room and stopped when she saw him. A lot of women would be repulsed by his scars. Not Caitlyn. She stared at his chest with frank curiosity before lifting her gaze to his face. "White or rye?"

"Did you get a good look?"

She shrugged. "I've seen worse."

Her attitude intrigued him. If he hadn't been desperate to get away from this area, he wouldn't have minded spending time with her, getting to know what made her tick. "Are you a nurse?"

"I used to be a reporter, embedded with the troops." She moved closer. "I know some basic first aid. I could take care of those cuts and bruises."

He didn't like asking for assistance, but the head wound needed attention. He went to his chair by the table and sat. "I got whacked on the back of my skull."

Without hesitation, she positioned herself behind him. Her fingers gently probed at the wound. "This looks bad, Jack. You should be in the hospital."

"No doctors."

"That's real macho, but not too smart." She stopped poking at his head and pulled a chair around so she was sitting opposite him. Their knees were almost touching. "I want you to look at my forehead. Try to focus."

"You're checking to see if my pupils are dilated."

"If you have a concussion, I'm taking you to the hospital. Head injuries are nothing to fool around with."

He did as she asked, staring at her forehead. Her eyebrows pulled into a scowl that she probably thought was tough and authoritative. But she was too damn cute to be intimidating. A sprinkle of freckles dotted her nose and cheeks. Her wide mouth was made for grinning.

In her blue eyes, he saw a glimmer of genuine concern, and it touched him. Though he couldn't remember his name or what kind of threat brought him to this cabin, he knew that it had been a long time since a woman looked at him this way.

She sat back in her chair. "What really happened to you? You didn't get that head injury in a car accident."

How could he tell her the truth? He didn't have the right to ask for her help; he was a stranger. She didn't owe him a damn thing. "I should go."

"Stay." She rested her hand on his bare shoulder. Her touch was cool, soothing. "I'll patch you up as best I can."

For the first time since he woke up this morning, he had the feeling that everything might turn out all right.

Chapter Three

Caitlyn only knew one thing for sure about Jack. He was stoic—incredibly stoic. His ability to tolerate pain was downright scary.

Moments ago, she'd closed the wound on his head with four stitches. Though she'd used a topical analgesic spray to deaden the area, the effect wasn't like anesthetic. And she wasn't a skilled surgeon. Her clumsy stitching must have hurt a lot.

He hadn't flinched. When she had finished, he turned his head and calmly thanked her.

After that, he had wanted to leave, but she insisted that he stay long enough to eat something and have some water. After sewing him back together, she was invested in his survival.

Also, she was curious—an occupational hazard for a journalist. She wanted to get Jack's true story.

They sat at her dining room table, and she watched as he devoured an egg salad on light rye. She'd found him a faded black T-shirt that belonged to her brother, who wasn't as big as Jack but wore his clothes baggy. The fabric stretched tight across Jack's chest. Underneath were all those scars. How had he gotten wounded? In battle? The long ridge of puckered flesh on his torso was still healing and couldn't have been more than a couple of months old.

If he'd been injured in military service, he wouldn't have been discharged so quickly.

She nibbled at her own sandwich, trying to find a non-intrusive angle that might get him talking. In her work, she'd done hundreds of interviews, some with hostiles. The direct question-and-answer approach wouldn't work with Jack.

"You're not from around here," she said, "What brought you to the mountains?"

"Beautiful scenery. Fresh air."

Spare me the travelogue. "Where did you grow up?"

"Chicago."

Was he a kid from the burbs or a product of the mean streets? Instead of pushing, she offered an observation of her own. "One of the best times I had in Chicago was sailing on Lake Michigan at dusk, watching as the lights of the city blinked on."

He continued to eat, moving from the sandwich to a mouthful of the beans she'd heated on the stove.

"Your turn," she said.

"To do what?"

"I tell you something about me, and then you share something about yourself. It's called a conversation."

His gaze was cool, unreadable and fascinating. The green of his eyes contained dark prisms that drew her closer. "You have questions."

"We're just having a chat. Come on, Jack. Tell me something about growing up in the Windy City."

"The El," he said. "I don't care for underground subways, but I always liked riding the elevated trains. The jostling. The hustle. Made me feel like I was going someplace, like I had a purpose."

"Where were you going?"

"To see Mark." As soon as he spoke, his eyebrows

pinched in a frown. He swallowed hard as though he wanted to take back that name.

"Is Mark a friend?"

"A good friend. Mark Santoro. He's dead."

"I'm sorry for your loss."

"Me, too."

His friend's name rang a bell for her. Even though she hadn't been following the news regularly, she knew that the Santoros were an old-time but still notorious crime family. For the first time in weeks, she glanced longingly at her laptop. Given a few minutes to research on the internet, she might be about to solve the mystery of Jack Dalton.

"I haven't been honest with you, Caitlyn."

"I know."

"I didn't have a car accident."

"What else?"

"There are some guys looking for me. They've got a grudge. When I came here, I thought I could use your car for a getaway. But that's not going to work."

"Not that I'm volunteering my SUV for your getaway, but what changed your mind?"

"If I have your car, it connects you to me. I don't want anybody coming after you."

She agreed. Being targeted by the Santoro family wasn't her idea of a good time. "We should call the police. I have a friend, Danny Laurence, who's a deputy sheriff. He's somebody you can trust."

"I'm better off on my own."

He rose from the table, and she knew he was ready to depart. She hated the thought of him being out there, on his own, against powerful enemies. She bounced to her feet. "Let me call Danny. Please."

"You're a good person, Caitlyn." He reached toward her. When his large hand rested on her shoulder, a magnetic pull urged her closer to him. Her weight shifted forward, narrowing the space between them. He leaned down and kissed her forehead. "It's best if you forget you ever saw me."

As if that would happen. There weren't a whole lot of handsome mystery men who appeared on her doorstep. For the past month, she'd been a hermit who barely talked to anyone. "You won't be easy to forget."

"Nor will you."

"For the record, I still think you need to go to the hospital."

"Duly noted."

From outside, she heard the grating of tires on gravel.

Jack had heard it, too. In a few strides, he was at the front window, peering around the edge of the curtain.

A 1957 vintage Ford Fairlane—two-toned in turquoise and cream—was headed down her driveway. She knew the car, and the driver was someone she trusted implicitly. His vehicle was followed by a black SUV with tinted windows. "Do you see the SUV? Are these the people who are after you?"

"Don't know," he said. "They've seen your car so you can't pretend you're not here. Go ahead and talk to them. Don't tell them you've seen me."

"Understood." She gave him a nod. "You stay in the house. I'll get rid of them."

Smoothing her hair back into her ponytail, she went to the front door, aware that she might be coming face-to-face with the enforcers for a powerful crime family. Panic fluttered behind her eyelids, and she blinked it away. This wasn't her first ride on the roller coaster. She'd gotten through war zones, faced terrorists and bloody death. A couple of thugs from Chicago shouldn't be a problem.

From the porch, she watched as the Ford Fairlane parked

near her back door. The black SUV pulled up to the rear bumper of her car before it stopped.

She waved to Bob Woodley—a tall, rangy, white-haired man who had been a longtime friend of her family. He was one of the few people she'd seen since moving back to the cabin. A retired English teacher, he had been a mentor to her when she was in her teens. "Hi, Mr. Woodley."

He motioned her toward him. "Get over here, Caitlyn. Give an old man a proper hello."

When she hugged him, he must have sensed her apprehension. He studied her expression. His bushy eyebrows pulled into a scowl. "Something wrong?"

"I'm fine." She forced a smile. "What brings you here?"

"I was visiting Heather at the Circle L when these two gentlemen showed up. Since I'm a state congressman, I figured it was my duty to extend a helping hand to these strangers by showing them how to find your cabin."

She looked past him toward the SUV. The two men walking toward her were a sinister contrast to Mr. Woodley's open honesty. Both wore jeans and sports jackets that didn't quite hide the bulge of shoulder holsters. Dark glasses shaded their eyes.

Woodley performed the introductions. "Caitlyn, I want you to meet Drew Kelso and Greg Reynolds."

When she shook their hands, their flesh was cold—either from the air-conditioning in their car or because they were reptiles. "What can I do for you?"

Woodley said, "We understand that you had a visitor this morning."

How did they know about Jack? Had her cabin been under surveillance? "I'm not sure what you're talking about."

"The dappled gray mare," Woodley said. "You had Heather come over and pick it up."

"Oh, the horse." She rolled her eyes in an attempt to look like a ditzy blonde. She didn't want these men to take her seriously, wanted them to dismiss her as harmless. "Silly me, I'd already forgotten about the horse."

The one named Reynolds said, "It belongs to someone we know."

"Your friend needs to be more careful," she said. "The horse showed up on my property without a saddle or a bridle or anything."

The friendly smiles she offered to the two thugs went unanswered. They meant business.

The taller, Drew, had sandy hair and heavy shoulders. His mouth barely moved when he spoke. "We're looking for the guy who was riding that horse."

"I didn't see anybody." She widened her eyes, even fluttered her lashes. "Like I said, no bridle or saddle."

Drew said, "If you saw him, it'd be smart to tell us."

His comment sounded a bit like a threat. "Who is this person? What's his name?"

"Tony Perez."

With complete honesty, she shook her head. "Never heard of him. But I'll be on the lookout. Is there a number I should call if I see him?"

Drew handed her a business card that contained only his name and a cell phone number.

"I guess that wraps up our business." Woodley checked his wristwatch. "I'd better shove off."

She wanted to cling to him and plead for him to stay until these two men were gone. "Can't you stay for coffee?"

"Sorry, kiddo. I'm running late for an appointment in Pinedale." He strolled toward his vintage Ford Fairlane. "I hope you gents can find your missing friend."

They gave him a nod and headed toward their SUV. Caitlyn breathed a little sigh of relief. They were leaving. The crisis was averted.

Before Woodley climbed behind the steering wheel, he said, "Don't be a stranger, Caitlyn."

He drove down her driveway and turned onto the road. The two men stood beside their SUV talking. With every fiber of her being, she wanted them gone. These were two scary guys. Why hadn't Mr. Woodley been able to see it?

They came back toward her. Drew said, "We want to take a look around. To make sure he's not hiding around here."

"That's not necessary." She positioned herself between him and her front porch. "There's nobody here but me."

Drew glanced over his shoulder at the other man, Greg Reynolds. He was neat and crisp. His boots were polished. His charcoal sports jacket showed expensive tailoring, and his thick black hair glistened in the sunlight. She guessed that he was a man of expensive tastes, definitely the boss.

Greg gave a slight nod, and Drew walked toward her cabin. Short of tackling him, there was no way Caitlyn could stop him. Still, she had to try.

"Hey." She grasped his arm. "I told you. There's nobody here."

Slowly, he turned toward her and removed his sunglasses. He didn't need to speak; the curl of his upper lip and the flat, angry glare from his eyes told her that he wouldn't hesitate to use violence. And he would most likely enjoy hurting her.

She stepped back. Silently, she prayed that Jack had hidden himself well or had managed to slip out the back door.

"This is for your own safety," Drew said. "Tony Perez is dangerous."

As she entered her cabin, her heart was pumping hard. She shoved her hands into her pockets so no one would notice the trembling.

Jack had cleaned up every trace of his presence. On the dining room table, there was only one plate and one bottled water. She watched as Drew went into the bathroom. Jack's discarded clothing had been in there. Apparently, his shirt and undershirt were gone because Drew emerged without saying anything.

When Tony brushed past her, she caught a whiff of his expensive cologne. It smelled like newly minted hundred-dollar bills. He rested his hand on the door handle of the front closet and yanked it open. She noticed that her rifle was gone.

IN THE LOFT ABOVE the stalls in the horse barn, Jack lay on his belly and sighted down the barrel of Caitlyn's rifle. This weapon lacked the sophistication of the sniper equipment he was accustomed to using. Her rifle scope was rudimentary and so poorly mounted that he had removed it. At this range, he trusted his marksmanship. His first shot would show him the correction for this particular weapon, after which he would be accurate.

His plan was simple. Take out the tall man with sandy hair; he was the most deadly. Then the boss.

Holding the rifle felt natural, and he easily comprehended the necessary strategy in an assault situation. These skills weren't inborn. He couldn't remember where he'd learned or who taught him. But he knew how to kill.

When Caitlyn and the men entered the house, Jack adjusted his position, trying to keep track of their movements through the windows. So far they hadn't threatened Caitlyn, except for that moment when she touched the sandy-haired thug. The bastard looked like he wanted to kill her. If he'd hurt her, Jack would have squeezed the trigger. He'd gotten Caitlyn into this mess, but he wouldn't let her be harmed.

The optimum scenario would be for them to make their search and then go. She wasn't a part of this.

Not being able to see what was going on inside the house made him edgy. If they didn't come outside soon, he needed to move in closer to protect her. He started a mental timer for five minutes.

In the corral below him, the two horses—one light and one dark—stood at the railing. Their ears pricked up. They nickered and shifted their hooves. Animals could sense when something was wrong. The horses knew.

He was nearing the end of his countdown when the small group emerged from the back door. Caitlyn looked angry. Earlier, she'd tried to act like a dumb blonde and had failed miserably. Her intelligence showed in every move she made and every word she spoke.

The two men walked ahead of her toward the barn. Jack got ready to shoot. His position gave him an advantage, but he needed to time his shot so there was no chance they could retaliate. He wished there was some way to signal Caitlyn to keep her distance from them.

They walked toward the corral. Coming closer, closer. They were less than fifty yards from his position. The tall man was in front. His hand slid inside his jacket, and he pulled his handgun.

Jack aimed for the center of his chest, the largest target. If he'd been using a more sophisticated weapon, he would have gone for a head shot.

He heard Caitlyn object. "What are you doing? Why do you have a gun?"

The other man assured her, "We have to be prepared. The person we're looking for is extremely dangerous."

Damn right. Jack knew he was capable of lethal action. A trained killer. *Damn it, Caitlyn. Get out of the way.* The slick-looking man with black hair, the boss, stayed close to her. Too close.

Jack adjusted his aim. He'd kill the boss first. As he stared, he realized that he knew this man. Gregorio Rojas. He was the younger son of a drug cartel family that supplied the entire Midwestern United States.

Hatred flared in Jack's gut. His finger tensed on the trigger. Rojas was his sworn enemy. *Take the shot. Rid the world of this bastard whose actions have been responsible for so much misery, so much death.*

Rojas paused, took a cell phone from his pocket. After a brief conversation, he motioned to the other man. They headed back toward their vehicle.

Still, Jack didn't relax his vigilance. Rojas was still within range.

His memory was returning. The blank spaces knitted together in a tapestry of violence. *Take the shot.*

Chapter Four

Jack knew he had killed before. As he stared down the barrel of Caitlyn's rifle, his vision narrowed to his target. The center seam of Rojas's tailored jacket. His hands were steady. He was focused. Cool and calm, as always.

He remembered another time, another place, another killing.

He was in the city, the seedy part of town. On the fourth floor of a dirty brick hotel that rented rooms by the hour, he set up his sniper's nest and assembled his precision rifle with laser scope, silencer and tripod. With high-power, infrared binoculars, he observed the crappy apartment building directly across the street. Fourth floor, corner unit. Nobody home.

He checked into the hotel at sundown. Hours passed. Dusk turned to nightfall when lights flickered on throughout the city. Not that he had a glittering view.

When the lamp in the apartment across the street came on, he eased into position. Though he sat in the dark, the glow from a streetlight reflected dully on the barrel of his rifle and silencer.

He peered through his scope. Through the uncurtained window of the apartment across the street, a man with fiery red hair paced from room to room with his gun in his hand, looking for danger.

"I'm here," Jack whispered. *"Come to the window, you bastard."*

This man deserved to die.

But his target hadn't been alone. A small woman with brassy blond hair and a child entered Jack's field of vision. Two witnesses.

The killing had to wait.

From the loft in the barn, Jack watched as Rojas and his companion got into the SUV and drove away from Caitlyn's cabin. She turned on her heel and rushed back into her house, moving fast, as though she had something burning on the stove.

When the black SUV was out of sight, he rolled onto his back and stared up at the ceiling in the barn that needed patching.

He knew who he was.

A stone-cold killer.

INSIDE HER CABIN, Caitlyn wasted no time. She dove into the swivel chair behind her small desk in the living room and fired up her laptop. It felt good to see the screen come to life. Back when she was a working journalist—especially in the field—her computer had been an ever-present tool, almost an extension of her arm.

Her hands poised over the keyboard. *But I'm not a journalist anymore. Not right now.* She had no assignment, no story to investigate, and she wasn't entirely sure that she wanted to go back into the fray.

Her main reason for moving to this cabin had been to purposely distance herself from the 24-hour-a-day news cycle. During this time of self-imposed seclusion, she hoped to regroup and decide what to do with the rest of her life.

Her parents and nearly everyone else who cared about her had encouraged Caitlyn to seek out a safer occupation.

Not that they wanted her to quit writing, but they hoped she would leave the war zones to others. As if she'd be satisfied reporting on garden parties? Writing poetry about sunshine and lollipops?

She wasn't made that way. She thrived on action.

Jack's arrival at her doorstep might be fate. She hadn't gone looking for danger, but here it was. She had armed thugs searching her cabin. If Jack Dalton had a story to tell, she wouldn't turn away.

She jumped on the internet and started a search on the name of Jack's supposed "friend," Mark Santoro. Expertly, she sorted through news stories, mostly from the *Chicago Tribune,* and put together the basic facts.

As Jack had said, Mark Santoro was dead. He and four other members of the Santoro crime family had been killed in a shootout on a city street five months ago. One of the men had his hands cut off. Mark had been decapitated. A gruesome slaughter; it was intended to send a message.

Allegedly, the Santoro family handled narcotics distribution in the Midwest, and they had angered the powerful Rojas drug cartel—the suppliers of illegal drugs.

Agents from the DEA and the Bureau of Alcohol, Tobacco, Firearms and Explosives were all over this incident. They arrested and charged several members of the Rojas cartel, including the top man, Tom Rojas. The federal murder trial was due to start on Tuesday, four days from now, at a district court in Chicago.

Reading between the lines, Caitlyn suspected that much of this story never made it to print. She used to date a reporter who worked at the *Trib*—a sweet guy who had taken her for that romantic sailboat ride on Lake Michigan and begged her to stay in the States. She'd refused to settle down, and he'd moved on. A typical pattern for her relationships. The last she'd heard, her former beau was happily married with an infant daughter. If she needed to find out more about the trial, she could contact him.

Rapid-fire, she typed in the names of the two thugs: Drew Kelso and Greg Reynolds. A quick search showed several people with those names, but nothing stood out. She wasn't surprised. Drug lords and thugs don't generally maintain websites.

Next, she searched for Tony Perez. After digging through a lot of worthless information, she tightened her search and linked it to Mark Santoro. In one of the articles about the shootings, Tony Perez was mentioned as a bodyguard for Santoro. Perez had been killed at the scene.

But Jack Dalton was very much alive.

Slowly, she closed her laptop. Though she hadn't heard him enter the house or walk across the living room floor, she sensed Jack's nearness. She knew that he was standing close, silently watching her.

A shiver prickled down her spine. She wasn't afraid that he would physically harm her. There wasn't a reason, and he was smart enough to avoid unnecessary violence. But she was apprehensive. Jack was pulling her toward a place she didn't want to go.

"Did you find what you were looking for?" he asked.

She swiveled in her desk chair to face him. "You look pretty healthy for a dead man."

He crossed the room and returned her rifle to the front closet. "I brought your gun back."

The smart thing would be to send him on his way and forget she ever saw him. But finding the truth was a compulsion for her. "Those men were looking for Tony Perez. Is that your real name?"

"Tony's dead. Call me Jack."

"They said you stole a horse, and that you're dangerous."

"Half right."

"Which half?"

"I didn't steal the horse. I borrowed it."

He approached her, braced his hands on each of the arms of her swivel chair and leaned down until his face was on a level with hers. "Those men are unpredictable. There's no telling what they might do. I strongly advise that you stay with a friend for a couple of days."

"What about you? Where are you going?"

"Not your problem."

He was so close that she could see the rise and fall of his chest as he breathed. She wanted to rest her hand against his black T-shirt, to feel the beating of his heart. Instead, she picked a piece of straw off his shoulder. "You were hiding in the barn. In the loft."

"I couldn't leave until I knew you were safe."

"Who were those guys?" She searched his eyes for a truth he might never tell her. "They said their names were Drew Kelso and Greg Reynolds."

"Not Reynolds. That was Gregorio Rojas." He reached toward her desk and flipped her computer open. "You know the name. You were reading all about him and his pals."

"And his brother, Tom. His murder trial starts in four days."

He stepped away from her. "I have to go."

"Not yet. I'm still putting the pieces together." She left her chair and stood between him and the front door. "I'm asking myself why Rojas is after you. Something to do with his brother's trial, right?"

"You don't need to know."

"But I do, Jack. I'm a reporter." And she was damn good at her job. He'd thrown out just enough bread crumbs for her to follow this trail. "Let's suppose that you are this

Tony Perez and that you survived the attack on the street. That makes you a witness."

"I told you before. Tony is—"

"Dead." *Yeah, sure.* "I'm just supposing here. I can only think of one reason that an eyewitness to a crime in Chicago would be hiding in the Colorado mountains. WitSec."

The Witness Security Program provided protection for those who might be in danger before a trial. There must be a safe house in the area.

"Suppose you're correct," he said. "If a protected witness was attacked at a safe house, it must mean that he was betrayed by the marshals who were supposed to be looking out for him. They gave the location of the safe house to Rojas."

She hated to acknowledge that law enforcement officials—in this case, U.S. Marshals—could be corrupted. But she knew it was possible. While embedded with the troops, she'd run across similar instances. Somebody taking a payoff. Somebody acting on a grudge instead of following orders.

With a shrug, she said, "It happens."

"If it did happen that way, there's nobody this witness can trust. Rojas is after him. And the marshals can't let him report them. He has to go on the run and find his own way to make it to the trial in Chicago."

"I can help you."

"I don't want your help."

He stepped around her and went out the front door.

JACK STRODE AWAY FROM her house toward the corral fence. Angry at himself for telling too much. Angry at her for wanting to know. How the hell could she help him? And why? Why should she give a damn? As a reporter with the troops, she was accustomed to being surrounded by heroes. Not somebody like him.

At the fence, he paused to settle his mind into a plan. He wasn't sure how he'd make his way out of this sprawling mountain terrain where a man could disappear and never be seen again. That might be the solution. *Drop out of sight and start over.*

But he had promised to appear in court. His eyewitness testimony would put Tom Rojas and some of his top men behind bars. Little brother Gregorio didn't have the guts or the authority to hold the cartel together. Jack's testimony could make a difference.

He looked toward the road that ran past her house—the only direct route into and out of this area. His enemies would be watching that road. He'd be better off taking a cross-country path, walking until… Until he got to Chicago?

"Jack, wait!" Caitlyn dashed toward him. She thrust a canvas backpack into his hands. "Take this."

Inside the pack, he saw survival supplies: a couple of bottled waters, some energy bars, a sweatshirt and a cell phone. He'd be a fool to refuse these useful items, but he wasn't going to admit that she'd been right about him needing her help.

She dug into the pocket of her jeans and pulled out a wad of cash. "It's a hundred and twenty-seven bucks. That's all I have on hand."

"Caitlyn, why—"

"And this." She handed him a cowboy hat. "To protect the wound on your head."

Jack tried on the battered brown hat with a flat brim. Not a bad fit. "Why are you so determined to help me?"

Her face was as open as a sunflower, deceptively innocent. "Why shouldn't I?"

"You don't know me. You don't know the life I've led."

"You were part of the Santoro crime family," she said. "I'm assuming that you've done a lot of things I wouldn't condone. You could have been a hit man, an assassin or even a drug pusher."

"No," he said, "never a pusher. I hate drugs."

"That's the past, Jack. You made a change. You decided to testify against some very bad men."

"Maybe I didn't have a choice."

"I don't care."

He was surprised to hear a tremble in her voice, an undercurrent of strong emotion. She was feeling something intense. About him? He didn't think she was the kind of woman who formed sudden attachments. Over and over, she'd said she was a reporter. In her profession, she couldn't allow her passions to rule. "What's going on with you?"

"You're risking your life to testify, to do the right thing." She inhaled so deeply that her nostrils flared. As she exhaled, she regained control of herself. "I need to believe that when people fight for the right thing and put their lives on the line, it's not for nothing. Their sacrifice has significance."

Spoken like someone who had been to war and had seen real suffering. His irritation faded behind a newfound admiration. She was one hell of a woman. Strong and principled. For the second time, he wished they had met under different circumstances. "Don't make me into something I'm not."

"Fair enough," she said. "As long as you don't downplay what you're doing. You're giving up your former life to do the right thing."

"I'm no hero."

She cocked her head to one side. A hank of straight blond hair fell across her forehead. "Neither am I."

"I have to go."

"First, let me show you how to use the GPS on the cell phone. It won't give you a detailed topographical map, but you'll have an idea where the roads are."

Instead, he handed the phone back to her. "If the GPS shows me where I am, it'll show other people my location. They can track me from the signal."

"Of course. I knew that." She shoved the phone into her pocket. "You said you didn't want to use my car, but you could take one of the horses."

On horseback, he'd make better time than if he was on foot. He nodded, accepting her offer. "I'll find a way to return the horse to you."

"You should take the stallion. His name is Fabio because of his blond mane. And he's a real stud."

Entering through the corral gate, she motioned to the handsome palomino horse and made a clicking with her tongue. Both animals responded and obediently trotted toward the barn door.

As he followed, he noticed her athletic stride. There was nothing artificial about her. No makeup. No fancy styling to her hair. Her body was well toned, and he suspected that her fitness came from outdoor living rather than a regular workout at a gym. Her jeans fit snugly, tight enough to outline the feminine curve of her ass.

Until now, he hadn't really taken the time to appreciate how attractive she was. When he first stopped at her cabin, he thought he'd be there for only a couple of minutes. He hadn't expected to know anything about her.

While she saddled the stallion and rattled off instructions for the care of the horse, he watched. Her energy impressed him. She was unlike any woman he'd known before. He regretted that after he rode away from her cabin, he would never see her again.

He harbored no illusions about coming back to her after the trial. His life wasn't his own. He'd be stashed away in witness protection, which was probably for the best. Right now, Caitlyn had a high opinion of him. If she knew the reality of his life, she wouldn't want to be in the same room with him.

She finished with the saddle and came toward him. "Fabio is ready to go."

"I'm not."

He placed his hand at the narrowest part of her body and gently pulled her closer.

Chapter Five

When Jack laid his hand possessively on her waist, Caitlyn knew what was coming next. Awareness gusted through her like a moist, sultry breeze that subtly pushed her toward him.

His green eyes shone with an unmistakable invitation, but he gave her plenty of time to back off and say no. During the past several years, she'd spent most of her days in the company of men and had learned how to make it clear that she wanted to spend her nights alone. But she wanted Jack to kiss her. His story had touched the very core of her being and reminded her of important truths. As if she wanted to kiss him because of her principles? *Yeah, right.* There was a whole lot more going on when she looked into Jack's handsome mug. The man was hot. Sexy as hell.

She leaned toward him. Her breasts grazed his chest as she tilted her head back. Her lips parted. Her eyelids closed.

The firm pressure of his mouth against hers started an earthquake inside her. She gasped, enjoying the tremors. Her arms wrapped around him, her body molded to his and she held on tight. It had been a long time since she felt so totally aroused. Way too long.

His big hands slid down her back and cupped her bottom.

He fitted her tightly against his hard body. The natural passion that she usually suppressed raced through her.

If they had more time, she would have gone to bed with him. But that was purely hypothetical. He had to depart immediately. Maybe that was why she could kiss him with such abandon. She knew she'd never see him again.

With obvious reluctance, he ended the kiss and stepped back. "I should go."

Every cell in her body wanted him. She struggled to be cool. "I wish you'd let me call my friend Danny."

"The deputy?"

She nodded vigorously, trying to ignore her intense desire and be logical. "After what you told me, I understand why you don't want to contact anybody in law enforcement. But I've known Danny since we were kids. I trust him."

"That's exactly why you shouldn't call him." He reached toward her and tucked a piece of hair behind her ear. "If he helped me, I'd be putting him and everyone he knows in danger."

"From Rojas," she said.

"You're a reporter. You know how the drug cartels deal with people who get in their way."

Though it was difficult to imagine grisly violence in the Colorado mountains under peaceful blue skies, she knew he was right. Revenge from the drug cartels was equal to the horrors she'd seen in the Middle East. Whole families—women and children—were brutally slaughtered, their bodies dismembered and left to rot.

Those images completely doused her desire. Jack had to go. He had to find his way to safety.

"I'm worried for you," she said. "I don't suppose you'd consider taking me along."

"Not a chance." He grinned, and she realized that it was

the first time she'd seen him crack a smile. "Why would you even ask?"

"A federal witness on the run? It's a damn good story."

"Not unless it has a happy ending."

He mounted the palomino stallion. Though Jack wasn't a cowboy, he looked real good on horseback. She hated that he was on the run, couldn't accept that she'd never be with him. There had to be a way to see him again.

Of course there is. She knew where the trial was taking place. If she pulled some strings and used her press credentials, she could wangle a seat inside the courtroom. "I'll see you in Chicago."

"If I make it."

With a wave, he rode from the barn.

She was left standing in the corral, watching as Jack rode into the forest behind her cabin. If she'd been riding beside him, she would have told him to go the other way. Across the meadow, he should have headed southeast. The terrain was less daunting in that direction, and there was water. Eventually, he would have found the Platte River. *What if he doesn't make it?*

Being left behind while someone else charged into danger wasn't the way she operated. She had to do something.

Taking the cell phone from her pocket, she called Heather to get her brother's phone number.

DANNY LAURENCE WASN'T as yummy as she remembered from her high school years. Though he looked sharp in his dark blue deputy uniform shirt, he was developing a bit of a paunch—a testament to being settled down and eating home-cooked meals every night.

He took off his cowboy hat as he sat at the head of her

dining room table. His short hair made his ears look huge. Had he always had those ears?

"Good to see you," he said. "I've been meaning to drop by and talk about old times."

"Same here. And I want to meet the woman who finally got Danny Laurence to take that long walk down the aisle."

"Sandra." He spoke her name fondly. "You'd like her. She's kind of a goofball."

"Is she Baby Blue or Green Light?"

He laughed. "It's been a long time since I heard those code words you and Heather made up to describe the guys you met. Baby Blue means a sissy, right? And Green Light is good to go."

"And Red Fire means trouble ahead." A particularly apt description. The English translation for *Rojas* was "red."

"My Sandra is Green Light all the way."

She was glad he'd found happiness. Not that a rosy future was ever in doubt; Danny had always been the most popular guy around—the captain of the football team, the president of the senior class.

Joining him at the table, she set a glass of fresh-squeezed lemonade in front of him. This was exactly the same seating arrangement she'd had with Jack, but the atmosphere was utterly different. With Danny, she felt friendly—as if they should tell dumb jokes and punch each other on the arm. There was none of the dangerous magnetism she experienced with Jack. The thought of him reminded her of their kiss and made the hairs on her arm stand up. Somehow, she had to help him.

She wished that she could come right out and ask Danny the questions she needed answered: Was there a WitSec safe house in the area? Did he know about a federal witness on the run? How could Jack be protected from a drug lord bent on revenge?

The direct approach wasn't an option. If Danny knew nothing, she wouldn't be the one to tell him and bring down the wrath of the Rojas. Caitlyn didn't want to be responsible for a bloodbath in Douglas County.

Danny took a swallow of lemonade. "What's up?"

"I was concerned about that horse I found." Jack had used the gray mare for his escape. Finding the owner meant locating the safe house. "Has anybody claimed her?"

"We haven't had a report of a stolen horse. Which isn't surprising. Livestock gets loose now and then. Nobody wants to make a big fuss only to have the horse come trotting back home."

"Have you checked the brand?"

"Not yet. A runaway horse isn't top priority. I've got other things to do."

"Such as?"

"The usual."

His attitude was way too laid-back to be dealing with the aftermath of a shootout at a WitSec safe house. She doubted that the marshals had reported Jack's disappearance, especially not if they were in collusion with Rojas. As far as she knew, federal marshals weren't required to check in with local law enforcement. It defeated the purpose of a safe house if too many people were aware of its existence.

"I was wondering," she said, "if there's been any kind of unusual activity around here?"

"Like what?"

"Oh, you know. Strangers in town. Suspicious stuff."

"You're working on some kind of news story, aren't you? You haven't changed a bit, Caitlyn. Always have to have the scoop." He sipped his lemonade and licked his lips. "Little Miss Know-It-All."

His teasing annoyed her. "You haven't changed, either. You're still the mean big brother, looking down his nose."

"I remember that time when you and Heather followed me and my date to a party in Bailey and I ended up having to escort you home. You two used to drive me crazy."

"Ditto." She actually did punch him on the arm. "Suppose I was working on a story. I'm not saying I am, just suppose. Would you have anything to tell me?"

"Could you be more specific?"

Not without putting him in danger. "I'm wondering if the FBI or maybe the federal marshals have any current operations in our area."

His expression turned serious. "If you have some kind of inside track on FBI activity, I want to hear about it."

"Nothing. I've got nothing."

"Why did you want me to come over?"

Aware that she'd already said too much, Caitlyn changed directions. "Do you know a guy named Jack Dalton?"

"As a matter of fact, I arrested that sorry son-of-a-gun last night at the Gopher Hole. Drunk and disorderly. He's sleeping it off in jail."

That solved the mystery of her missing handyman—the *real* Jack Dalton. "I almost hired him to work for me."

"Aw, hell, Caitlyn. Don't tell me this Dalton character is some kind of FBI agent."

"He's just another troubled soul." And not her responsibility. "When he wakes up, tell him he lost the job."

"You're acting real weird. You want to tell me what's wrong?"

"I'm just nervous. Because of the horse." She thought about mentioning the two armed thugs and decided against it. There wasn't anything Danny could do about them. "Lately, I've been jumpy."

As he studied her, his expression changed from irritation to something resembling compassion. He reached over and gently patted her arm. "Heather told me that you'd been through a lot, reporting on the war. She's kind of worried about you."

The last thing she wanted was pity. "I'm fine."

"It's okay to be nervous."

"I told you. I'm doing just fine."

"Whatever you say." He drained his glass of lemonade, stood and picked up his hat. "I want you to know, it's all right for you to call me any time."

"If I run into any Red Fire situations, I'll let you know."

He stepped outside onto the porch and waited for her to join him. "The sheriff just hired a new guy who was in Iraq. He happens to be single. If you want to talk, he'd—"

"Whoa." She held up her hand. "I never thought I'd see the day when Danny Laurence started playing matchmaker."

"That's what happens when you get settled down. You want everybody else to pair up."

"When I'm ready to jump into the singles pool, I'll let you know."

"Fair enough."

"Thanks for coming over." She gave him a warm smile. "Be careful, Danny."

"You, too."

She watched as he drove away in his police vehicle with the Douglas County logo on the side. Asking him to come here hadn't given her any new information, except to confirm the identity of Jack Dalton. The *real* Jack Dalton was not the man who had showed up on her doorstep. *Her* Jack

Dalton was actually Tony Perez. But he didn't want to use that name. Because he'd changed? She wanted to believe that when Tony Perez agreed to testify, he abandoned his old life.

Her gaze wandered to the hillside where she'd last seen him. By now he'd be miles away from here.

She missed him.

For that matter, she also missed the real Jack Dalton. Without a handyman, patching the barn roof was going to be nearly impossible. *Who cares?* Did it really matter if her barn leaked? Earlier today, she'd thought so.

For the past weeks, she'd filled her waking hours with projects—cleaning, painting, doing chores and making repairs. Those jobs now seemed like wasted energy. Not like when she'd been talking to Jack, figuring out his identity. Tracking down a story made her feel vital and alive. At heart, she was a journalist. That was what she needed to be doing with the rest of her life.

Her decision was made. The time had come for her self-imposed seclusion to end. Looking across the road, she scanned the wide expanse of sagebrush and prairie grass that led to the rugged sweep of forested hillsides. A rich, beautiful landscape, but she didn't belong here.

Her job was to follow the story. Packing a suitcase would take only a couple of minutes; she was accustomed to traveling light. She could be on her way in minutes, driving toward Denver International Airport, where she could catch the next flight to Chicago.

But what if Jack ran into trouble and came back to the cabin? She needed to stay, if only for twenty-four hours. As long as she was here, she might as well patch the barn roof.

She went back into the cabin and picked up her tool belt. Though she never locked her house when she was home, the recent threats emphasized the need for security. After she'd locked the front and back doors, she headed toward the barn.

The midday sun warmed her shoulders. Her life here was idyllic, but it wasn't where she needed to be. Why had she doubted herself? It was so obvious that she was a reporter. What was she afraid of? *Oh, let's see. A million different things.* Not that she was Baby Blue—a sissy. She'd always been brave, and living in a war zone had hardened her to the sight of blood and gore. She had faced unimaginable horror, and she'd learned to stifle her terror. But those fears never truly went away.

Though she'd never told anyone, she had experienced fits of uncontrolled sobbing, nightmares, even delusions. Once, she'd heard a helicopter passing overhead and panic overwhelmed her. She'd dropped to her knees and curled into a ball. Her mind wasn't right; she wasn't fit to be on the front line.

But she could still be a reporter; not every assignment required her to rush headlong into danger.

Inside the barn, she fastened the tool belt around her hips and looked up at the roof. One of the holes was so big that she could see daylight pouring through.

From the stall nearest the door, the bay mare snorted and pawed at the earthen floor.

"Oh, Lacy." Caitlyn went toward the horse. "I'm sorry. We missed our morning ride. Maybe later, okay?"

Lacy tossed her head as though angry. When she looked sadly at the empty stall beside her, Caitlyn felt guilty. Poor Lacy had been left behind, locked in her stall and deprived of her morning exercise.

"All right," Caitlyn said, "a short ride."

She had just gotten the horse saddled when she looked out the front door of the barn and saw the black SUV approaching her driveway. Rojas was back.

Chapter Six

After Jack left Caitlyn's cabin, he continued to discover more of his innate skills. Horseback riding wasn't one of them. Every time he urged Fabio into a pace faster than a walk, Jack bounced around in the saddle like a broken marionette. How did cowboys do this all day? His ass was already sore.

Lucky for him, Fabio was a genius. The big palomino responded to his clumsy tugging on the reins with impressive intelligence as they wove through the pines and leafy shrubs in the thick forest. They found a creek where the horse could drink, and a couple of rock formations that could be used for hideouts.

After getting repeatedly poked in the arms by branches, Jack put on the sweatshirt Caitlyn had so thoughtfully packed for him. He hadn't expected her help. Her kindness. Or her kiss. It meant something, that kiss. Beyond the pure animal satisfaction of holding a woman in his arms, he'd felt a stirring in his soul as though they were deeply connected. He had a bright fleeting memory of what it was like to be in love, but the thought quickly faded into the darker recesses of his mind.

There could never be anything significant between him and Caitlyn. If he survived the next four days and made it to the trial, he'd have a new life in witness protection. And it wouldn't include her.

Looking up at the sky through scraggly branches, Jack noted the position of the sun and determined which way was north. This ability to get his bearings came from outdoor training in rugged, arid terrain. He remembered a desert. And an instructor who spoke only Spanish and—surprise, surprise—Jack was able to translate. He was bilingual. Another useful skill.

Also, he had a sharp comprehension of strategy. He knew that Rojas and his men were looking for him, as were the marshals at the safe house who had betrayed him. They might have access to advanced technology. Though Jack didn't see or hear a chopper overhead, it was entirely possible that this whole area was under aerial surveillance. His plan was to stay under the cover of the trees until nightfall.

He headed northwest, roughly following the direction of the horse trailer he'd seen on the road to Caitlyn's cabin. The logo on the side of that truck said: Circle L Ranch, Pinedale, Colorado. Locating the nearby population center could prove useful, and Fabio seemed to know where they were going. The big horse moved smoothly through the forest until they came to a ridge overlooking a meadow.

From this vantage point, Jack looked down on a small herd of fat black cattle, twenty-five or thirty head. As he watched, cowboys in a truck pulled up to a feeding area. Another ranch hand on a dirt bike joined them. None of these men were on horseback.

Jack patted Fabio's neck beneath his flowing blond mane. "Don't worry, buddy. A truck will never replace you. You're too pretty."

For a moment, he considered riding down and asking for shelter. On a ranch, there would be a number of places to hide. But he didn't want to put these people in danger. If Rojas suspected they were helping him, he'd gun down every person on the ranch and probably shoot the cattle as well. Fear was how the cartel ran their business; violence was their methodology.

Had Mark Santoro been the same way? Jack had respected Mark. He liked him, but that didn't mean either of them were upstanding citizens.

A clear thought unfurled inside his head. *No crime justifies taking the law into your own hands.* He believed this principle. At the same time, he knew that he had violated it. He had performed an execution. The circumstance wasn't clear, but Jack had killed an unarmed man.

He tugged on Fabio's reins, and they went back into the forest, heading toward Caitlyn's cabin. Thinking about Rojas made him worry. What if the thugs returned to her place? Gregorio Rojas was notorious for taking rash action. He lashed out violently. If he couldn't find another lead, he might return to Caitlyn with the idea that he could make her talk. Even if she didn't know anything. Even if she was innocent.

With Fabio tethered to a tree, Jack settled down to watch the cabin. An open space in a roughly triangular shape stretched downhill to her back door. The back of the barn was only a couple hundred yards away. Leaning against a sun-warmed boulder, he opened one of the bottled waters and ate a crunchy energy bar. A full meal would be nice. A rare steak with baked potato. Maybe a nice Chianti. And a cigar.

The memory of those rich flavors teased his palate. His mouth watered. The rest of his past was sketchy, but he knew what he wanted for his last meal. He inhaled the remembered fragrance of mellow tobacco. A Cuban cigar, of course.

When he saw the police vehicle arrive at Caitlyn's cabin, he supposed this was the friend she kept talking about. Danny the deputy appeared to be a tall, good-looking guy. Standing on the porch, he gave her a hug that lasted a bit longer than a casual greeting. A boyfriend? Hopefully, she wouldn't feel compelled to tell Danny Boy all about him. The last thing Jack needed was the local cops putting out an APB. There were enough people after him already.

Jack was disappointed to see Danny drive away by himself. If Caitlyn had gone with him, she'd be safe. At least, she'd have an armed cop at her side.

Alone, she was vulnerable.

He considered sneaking down the hill and telling her to come with him. *Bad idea.* With him, she'd be in danger for sure. Without him, she had a chance. *Sit tight. This might all go away.*

Caitlyn seemed to be getting back to her routine. She came out the back door carrying her tool belt. Her single-minded determination made him grin; nothing was going to stop her from patching that roof.

He almost relaxed. Then he saw the black SUV. They were driving too fast on the two-lane gravel road. Reckless. Dangerous.

He had to get Caitlyn out of there. He pushed himself to his feet and ran. Instinctively, he dodged and stooped, staying away from the open area, keeping his approach camouflaged.

The SIG was in his hand. He'd checked the clip and knew he had only four bullets. That should be enough. If he got to the rear of the barn, he'd be in range. First, he'd take out the big bodyguard, the guy who called himself Drew Kelso. Then, he'd shoot Rojas.

The SUV parked in her driveway. Four men and Rojas

emerged. Five targets and only four bullets. Jack didn't like the odds.

Kelso led the way. The bodyguard yanked his handgun from the shoulder holster as he stormed toward the cabin. He yelled, "Hey, bitch. Get out here."

The others followed.

The fact that Caitlyn was in the barn might save her. If she moved fast enough, she could get away without having them notice.

Jack crouched at the edge of the trees. There was no cover between him and the back wall of the barn. He stared at the weathered wood. No back door. That would have been too easy.

Caitlyn came through the big door in the front. She was astride the bay mare and, for some reason, wearing her tool belt. If she rode toward the corral gate, it would bring her closer to Rojas. She wheeled the horse in the opposite direction—toward where he was hiding in the trees—and rode across the fenced corral. At the far end was a gate that opened into the field.

She rode straight at it, leaning forward in the saddle and moving fast. Her expertise in handling her mount was obvious, and he admired her skill.

Rojas and his men hadn't spotted her. They were occupied with breaking into her cabin, yelling threats. Jack hoped they would keep up their posturing until she'd gotten safely away.

He sprinted down the rugged hill. When he got to the gate, he'd throw it open. And she'd ride through to safety. Caitlyn was close, almost there. *Come on, baby, you can make it.*

The shouting from the cabin changed in tone. Like hunting dogs on the chase, they'd seen their quarry and reacted.

In front of the others, Kelso ran from her house toward the corral. Gunfire exploded in wild bursts.

Caitlyn stiffened in the saddle. She reined her horse. What the hell was she doing?

He reached the gate, unfastened the latch and threw it open. "Caitlyn," he called to her. "This way. Hurry."

She turned her head toward him. All the color had drained from her skin. Her mouth was open, gasping. Had she been hit?

At the other end of the corral, he saw the five men pour through the gate, waving their guns, yelling, shooting.

Jack wanted to return fire, but he only had four bullets. Every shot had to count.

Kelso stopped and spread his legs in a shooter's stance. With both hands, he took aim.

Jack dropped to one knee, pointed the SIG and squeezed the trigger.

His bullet found its mark. Kelso roared in pain, clutched his thigh and toppled to the dirt inside the corral.

The men behind him stumbled to a halt. They'd thought they were dealing with an unarmed woman. Hadn't expected to be in danger.

Taking advantage of their momentary confusion, Jack fired a second time. Again, he aimed for the legs. Another man screamed and fell.

The others were in retreat. The cowards didn't know he had only two bullets left. He took advantage. Grabbing the reins on Caitlyn's horse, he pulled her toward the open gate.

"Wait." Her voice quavered. "Mount up behind me."

He didn't question her or argue. On horseback, their chances for escape were a hell of a lot better. As she scooted forward and out of the saddle, he stuck his toe into the stirrup and took her place.

Riding like this wouldn't be easy. He would have preferred holding his ground and shooting, picking them off one by one. But he didn't have the firepower. Jack dug in his heels, urging the horse forward. They made it through the gate.

"Where are we going?" she asked.

"Uphill," he said. "Take cover in the trees."

Behind his back, he heard another couple of shots. Leaning forward, he wrapped his arms around her. A screwdriver handle from her tool belt dug into his gut. He noticed that with every blast of gunfire, her body trembled.

They made it into the forest.

When he looked over his shoulder toward the barn, he saw Rojas, staring after them. Revenge was all he lived for. The bastard wouldn't quit until Jack was dead. And now, Caitlyn was another object for his hatred.

Jack felt like hell. It was his fault that she was in danger. Because of him, her peaceful life was torn to shreds. This counted as one of the worst things he'd done in his life as Tony Perez or whoever he was.

"Where's Fabio?" she asked.

"Up here. To the right."

Still within earshot of the shouting from her cabin, they approached the tree where he'd tethered the horse. The big palomino nickered a greeting to the bay mare.

Jack dismounted and went to his horse while she readjusted her position. She reached down to the tool belt. "Should I take this off?"

"Keep it." Some of those tools might be modified to use as weapons. "Never can tell when you might need a ratchet."

"I think we should go to the Circle L."

Though her voice was still shaky, the blush had returned to her cheeks. He didn't know what had happened to her when the shooting started, but the intensity of her reaction gave him cause for worry. It was almost like she'd gone into shock.

"We can't involve anyone else," he explained. "If the people at the Circle L help us, they'll be in as much danger as we are. Follow me."

Disappearing in this vast wilderness wouldn't be difficult, but hiding the horses presented a problem. Not only did they need to locate a cave big enough for Fabio and Lacy but they had to figure out a way to keep the animals quiet.

He turned to her and asked, "Do you have your car keys?"

"Why?"

"We might need to use your car."

"The keys are in my pocket. It's weird. I don't usually lock my cabin. For some reason, I did."

"Your instinct was right. The locked doors slowed down Rojas and his men. It gave you more time to escape."

"Oh, damn," she muttered. "I'll bet they kicked in my door. That's going to be a problem. You know, I've gone to a lot of trouble fixing up the place."

Her attitude puzzled him. Earlier, she'd frozen in terror. Now, she seemed more concerned about property damage than the fact that she was running for her life. "A broken door is the least of your problems. Rojas and his men are more likely to burn your cabin to the ground."

"That's terrible. A wildfire would devastate miles of forest." Her blue eyes snapped. "But I guess drug cartels aren't real concerned about environmental damage."

He couldn't believe she was composed enough to make a joke. Every muscle in his body was tense. Their plodding progress along the path beside the creek was driving him crazy. He wanted to fly, but they couldn't go faster without heading into open terrain. It was safer to stay within the shelter of the forest.

Single file, they ascended a ridge leading away from the creek. Direct sunlight hit Fabio's mane. The golden horse glowed like a beacon. "We have to ditch the horses. What will they do if we dismount and continue on foot?"

"They'll probably trot along behind us."

Exactly what he was afraid of. They were approaching an area he'd explored earlier. A rugged granite cliff rose above the tree line. If they climbed those rocks, there were a number of crannies where they could hide until nightfall.

"I have an idea," she said. "Fabio and Lacy don't actually belong to me. They're from the Circle L. If we get within sight of the ranch and shoo them away, they'll probably trot home to their stable."

"I told you before. We can't drag anybody else into danger." Why didn't she understand? "If the horses show up, the people at the ranch will know that something happened to you. They'll report it. Local police will be involved."

"As if that's a bad thing?"

Her sarcasm was the last straw. He wheeled around on Fabio and rode up beside her, confronting her face-to-face. She appeared to be blasé and cool.

"There's a time to be a smart-ass, Caitlyn. This isn't it."

"What do you want me to do? Burst into tears?"

Tears would be more normal than the facade she was putting up. He wanted an honest reaction from her. "Rojas wants us dead. Both you and me. If he gets his hands on us, death won't be painless. This isn't a game. It isn't a tidy little story you're writing for an article."

"You don't know anything about what I do for a living."

"Tell me," he challenged.

"I lived on the front lines of battle." Her eyes darkened. She wasn't joking, not anymore. "I've seen things you couldn't imagine."

"There's a difference between reporting on the shooting and being the target."

"Really? The incoming bombs didn't know the difference. An improvised explosive device couldn't tell that I was a reporter. I know what it's like to be in danger, Jack. I remember every minute, every horrible minute. Sometimes, I wake up at night and…"

He was beginning to understand her earlier reaction. "That's what happened to you when you heard the gunfire. You had a flashback. You froze."

"The only way I can handle the panic is to ignore it, pretend that it's erased. But it won't go away. I can't forget. That fear is branded into my brain."

If they were going to survive, he needed for her to be fully in control. She needed to be smart and conscious. To get beyond the flashbacks.

If they weren't careful, her memories would kill them.

Chapter Seven

Caitlyn couldn't help feeling the way she did. Her way of hiding fear was bravado. Cracking jokes and making snide comments gave her a buffer zone. One of the reporters she worked with in Iraq said that when it came to gallows humor she was the executioner. What else could she do? The alternative was to turn as hard as stone.

But the way she'd frozen when she heard gunfire wasn't typical. In other combat situations, she'd been able to respond and follow orders. The attack at her cabin had been unprovoked, unexpected. Because there hadn't been time to prepare herself, fear rushed in and overwhelmed her. She could never let that happen again. Her response had almost gotten them killed.

Jack reached toward her, spanning the space between their horses. She slapped his hand and turned her head away. "I'm fine."

"Listen to me, Caitlyn."

"You don't have to explain again. I've read the news stories. I know the cartels are famous for their vengeance. And brutal. Their victims are dismembered, beheaded, burned alive. I know what Rojas is capable of."

"Look at me."

Reluctantly, she lifted her gaze. His eyes narrowed to

jade slits. A muscle twitched in his jaw. He was fierce, a warrior. Quietly, she said, "I'm glad you're on my side."

"I don't make promises lightly." His voice had an edge of steel. "Believe me, Caitlyn. I won't let them hurt you."

How could he stop them? Sure, he was tough, and his marksmanship at the cabin had been nothing short of amazing, but he was only one man. "We need backup."

"Do you really think your friend Danny is a match for Rojas?"

"What do you know about Danny?"

"I'm assuming he's the cop who came to your house."

"You were watching my cabin." She appreciated his concern. Instead of putting miles between himself and Rojas, Jack stuck around to keep an eye on her. "Why?"

"Guilt," he said. "I feel like hell for putting you in danger."

"How did you know they'd come back?"

"I didn't. That was the worst-case scenario." His eyes scanned the forest impatiently. "I have a strategy. Plan for the worst and hope for the best."

"Something you learned while working for Santoro?"

"Santoro wasn't my first job. Let's get back to Danny. You gave him a long hug. Are you close?"

"I've known him since we were teenagers. He's like a big brother. And why do you care about who I'm hugging? Are you jealous?"

"Hell, no."

His denial came too fast. *He was jealous.* "Danny is happily married."

"Good for him. Now, here's the plan. We'll take the horses down to a field and leave them. Then we come back here, climb the rocks and find a place to hide until nightfall."

"I know this area better than you," she said. "Let me take the lead."

"Move fast."

As she rode down to an open area beyond a grove of aspen, she digested the very interesting fact that Jack cared enough about her to stay and watch her cabin, and he was jealous when he saw another man give her a hug. He must be attracted to her. He'd kissed her, after all.

Frankly, that attraction went both ways. He was handsome, aggressive, masculine and…totally unavailable. It was just her rotten luck to get involved with a guy who worked for a crime family and would be going into witness protection.

When they reached the creek at the edge of the meadow, she dismounted, removed the saddles and used a rope to lightly hobble the front legs of their horses. She didn't like to leave Fabio and Lacy alone for a prolonged period of time, but they'd be all right for a couple of hours. When she and Jack were safely on their way, she'd call Heather and tell her where to find the horses.

Jack slung the little backpack she'd prepared for him over his shoulder. "Give me the tool belt," he said. "We're going to be moving fast, and it's heavy."

She unbuckled the belt and held it toward him. "How much time do we have before they come after us?"

"Not much." While he fastened the belt around his hips, he transferred his gun to his hand. "They had to deal with two injured men and arrange for off-road transportation. Those things take time, but I'm assuming they're already on our trail."

She swallowed the fear that was bubbling inside her. "I suppose that's the worst-case scenario."

"Getting caught is the worst." He looked back toward the rocky cliffs. "Stay under the cover of the trees."

"Why?"

He gestured to the cloudless blue skies overhead. "Possible aerial surveillance."

He really was thinking of every contingency. "Really?"

"Start running," he said.

Though she didn't follow a regular exercise routine, Caitlyn was in good physical condition. She jogged at the edge of the forest, dodging between the tree trunks and ducking under low-hanging branches. The vigorous motion got her heart pumping. Though breathing heavily, she wasn't winded. After a month at the cabin, the altitude didn't bother her. But Jack probably wasn't acclimated to the thin air at this elevation. She glanced over her shoulder to check on him.

With the gun in his hand and ferocious determination written into every line of his face, he showed no indication of being tired. "Faster," he said.

"Need to be careful." She took a breath. "Don't want to trip. Sprain an ankle."

"You can move faster."

She spurred herself forward. When her family spent summers at the cabin, she and her brother climbed all over these rocks and hills. She knew the perfect place to hide. Her thigh muscles strained as she started the final uphill push.

Pausing, she caught her breath. "We'll climb down this sharp ravine, then up and over those boulders."

"Right behind you."

Her hideout wasn't actually a cave; it was a natural cavern formed by huge chunks of granite piled against each other. The most dangerous part was at the top. She flattened her back against the rock and crept along a ledge. "Be careful here. The drop wouldn't kill you, but it'd hurt."

Even with the tool belt, he managed easily.

At the far side of the ledge, she slipped through a slit between two boulders and climbed down, placing her feet carefully. A cool shadow wrapped around her.

She was inside a low cavern. The waters of the creek trickled through the rocks above and formed a pool, which then spilled down into another cavern that wasn't visible from where she crouched on a rock.

Jack sat beside her. There wasn't enough room for him to stretch his legs out straight without getting his feet wet in the pool. "You did good, Caitlyn. This cave is excellent."

Sunlight through the slit provided enough illumination for her to see him. When she sat on the rock beside the pool, she felt moisture seeping into her jeans. "The only way they can find us is to stick their heads down here. Have you got any bullets left?"

"Two." He unbuckled the tool belt and moved closer to her. "The sound of the creek will cover our voices if we talk quietly."

Her muscles tingled from the run, and his nearness started a whole other spectrum of sensation. In spite of the danger and the fear, she was thinking of how good it would feel to lean against him and have his arm wrapped around her shoulders.

He pointed toward the ledge where the water made a miniature Niagara Falls. "There's another cavern below this one, right?"

"Two others. A large one that can be reached by following the creek. Then another. Then this cubbyhole."

"How visible is the approach to the first cavern?"

"If they come after us on horseback, they'd have to dismount and walk in. Rojas didn't impress me as the kind of man who did that kind of search."

"We have to remember the other men at the safe house," he said, "the federal marshals who betrayed me."

She hated to think of that conspiracy but didn't have trouble believing it had happened the way Jack said. Rojas had plenty of money to use as an enticement. "After you were found dead, how do you think the marshals planned to cover it up?"

"They could say that unidentified men in masks burst into the safe house and grabbed me. Or they could claim that I turned on them and they had to shoot me."

"What about me? How can they explain killing me?"

In the dim light, the rugged lines of his face seemed softer. The rough stubble on his chin faded to a shadow. "Your death wouldn't be explained. You'd just disappear. There's no tangible link between us."

"Yes, there is. The gray mare." The horse that showed up on her doorstep belonged to the men at the safe house. "A good investigator would connect the horse to my disappearance. Plus, Rojas and his men tore up my cabin. Somebody would have to suspect foul play."

"They'd blame it on me." His quiet words blended into the rushing of the creek. "Or on the unidentified men who killed me. The marshals wouldn't necessarily come under suspicion."

Though Rojas and his men represented a direct threat, she was more concerned with those federal marshals. They wouldn't charge through her door with guns blazing. Their approach would be subtle and clever. "What if they contact Danny to help them search for me? He knows about this cavern. He could lead them to us."

"Think it through," Jack said. "In the first place, they won't want to involve local law enforcement. Not while Rojas is in the area."

Wishing that she felt safer, she leaned against him. The warmth of his body contrasted with the cool surface of the rocks. His arm slipped around her.

She looked up at him. Would he kiss her again? Though she wouldn't mind a repeat, she was too nervous to relax and enjoy the sensations. "How long do we wait?"

"After dark," he said, "we'll go to your cabin and take your car."

"Won't they be watching?"

"I'll know if they are."

He sounded so confident that she believed him, even though she had no reason to think that he was a surveillance expert. Being in the employ of the Santoro family meant he knew his way around firearms and was probably good with his fists. But he seemed to have a wider spectrum of experience.

"I don't know much about you." In the subtle light of the cave, she studied him. "You might say I don't know Jack."

"Funny." He touched the tip of her nose with his index finger. "And this is an appropriate time for a joke."

"So glad I can entertain you. Seriously, though. Do you have training in surveillance?"

"I watched your cabin for over an hour, and you didn't know I was there."

"True, but I wasn't looking for you."

"I know how to shadow, how to observe and how to do a stakeout. And I learned from an expert. An old man who lived in Arizona. He was a tracker, a hunter. He showed me how to disappear in plain sight and how to sense when someone was coming after me."

"Sensing a threat? How does that work?"

"Awareness." He pointed to a glow that flickered against the cavern wall. "That patch of light is rising from the cave below us. If I see a shadow, I'll know that someone is approaching and getting too close."

She nodded. Though his method was simple, it hadn't occurred to her. "What else?"

"Listen to the rippling of the water as it slips from this cave to the next. There's a pattern to the sound. A splash indicates an obvious disturbance, but even a stealthy approach can be heard."

Though she concentrated on the sound of the water, she only heard gurgling and dripping. "This awareness thing is a kind of Zen-like approach. Was your teacher a guru?"

"He'd never use that word, but yes." Jack rattled off a sentence in Spanish, then he translated: "Wisdom comes from an open mind and profound simplicity."

"You speak Spanish. Are you from Mexico?"

"Does it matter?"

"Not really." When she shrugged, her shoulder rubbed against his chest. The moist air in the cavern sank into her pores like a cool sauna. "You make me curious. How did you get those scars on your chest?"

"How do you think?"

"You're being deliberately evasive." And it was beginning to irritate her. "There's no reason for you to be secretive. I already know you're not the real Jack Dalton, because Danny told me he's sleeping off a drunk-and-disorderly charge in jail. I know you're a federal witness on the run. And I'm fairly sure that you're Tony Perez."

"I guess you know it all."

She doubted that she'd even begun to scratch the surface of this complicated and somewhat infuriating man. "When I ask a question, I want an answer. How did you get those scars?"

"I was in a motorcycle accident. And a knife fight. Twice I was shot."

He'd lived a dangerous life, but she'd known that. "What were the circumstances? Why were you injured?"

"I have enemies. They don't place nice."

"Enemies like Gregorio Rojas and his brother," she said.

With his thumb he tilted her chin so she was looking up at his face. Though his expression was unreadable, his eyes glimmered, and that shine was somehow reassuring. A few years ago she had interviewed a mercenary in Afghanistan and had seen a flat coldness in his eyes, as though his soul no longer inhabited his body. Jack wasn't like that. Though she had no doubt that he'd killed people, he still had a conscience.

The tension in his jaw relaxed as he leaned closer to her. She arched her neck and closed her eyes, waiting for his kiss. His lips pressed firmly against hers. He withdrew an inch, then tasted her mouth more thoroughly, nibbling at her lower lip and gliding his tongue across her teeth.

His subtlety tantalized her, and she pressed for a harder, deeper kiss. This wasn't wise. Not profoundly simple. But she experienced a wonderful awareness.

He tensed and pulled away. Without speaking, he pointed to the patch of light on the wall. The pattern had changed. She heard a difference in the splashing of the water.

Someone had entered the cave below them.

Chapter Eight

Moving cautiously so he wouldn't betray their hiding place by scraping his boot against the rock, Jack positioned her in the darkest corner of the cavern. He figured that if she froze in panic, he wouldn't have to maneuver around her. Though he didn't dare peek over the ledge overlooking the lower cavern, he stretched out flat on his belly on the rock beside the water. If the searcher got close, Jack could react effectively. The SIG was in his hand.

A voice echoed from the cavern below them. "This is a good hiding place. Not big enough for their horses, though."

Another voice responded from a distance. "Do you see anything?"

A beam from a flashlight reflected on the wall and ceiling of the lower cave. Jack wished that he'd done more reconnaissance. Should have explored the cave below them. Should have been more prepared.

Glancing toward Caitlyn, he saw her tension, but she wasn't frozen as she'd been when she heard the gunfire. She managed a nod. Her eyes were huge. Her hands clenched at her breast.

From below he heard a splash.

"Damn," the voice said, "I got my boots wet."

"Any sign of them?"

"Nothing."

"We'll move on. They're on horseback and would have gone farther away from the cabin than this."

Jack listened carefully to their voices. One of them had a Texas twang that sounded familiar.

The flashlight beam went dark. There was the sound of more splashing from the lower caves. As the searchers moved away from them, his voice faded. "Here's what I don't understand. If he was at that woman's house, he'd have access to a phone. Why didn't he call for backup?"

Jack strained to hear what they were saying. Why did they think he could call for backup? The Santoros were based in Chicago. They couldn't help him from halfway across the country.

"Who knows what's going on in his head," said the other voice. "We're not dealing with an average person. He's a legend."

"Yeah, I've heard. Tall tales," the Texan drawled. "They say he hid out for six weeks in a jungle before he completed his mission."

Though the men were still talking, they were outside the cave. Jack could hear only bits and pieces of their conversation. Something about a "loner" and "killed a man."

He didn't remember surviving in a jungle. What kind of mission had he been on? Reaching into his memory was like sticking his hand into a grab bag. He didn't know whether he'd pull out a gold medal or a piece of dung.

When he felt Caitlyn touch him, he rolled onto his back and looked up at her. He knew that she'd heard as much as he had. Therefore she'd have questions. Even if he'd known all the answers, Jack figured it wasn't wise to go into details. Some memories were better left unsaid.

He sat up. She was close to him, kneeling on the rock

beside his thigh. Her jaw was tight. In a barely audible whisper, she asked, "Are they gone?"

He nodded. "We're safe. For now."

Exhaling in a whoosh, she sat back on her heels. He had the sense that she'd been holding her breath the whole time the searcher had been in the cave below them. Still whispering, she asked, "What did they mean when they said you could call for backup?"

Damned if I know. Hoping he could defuse her curiosity, he grabbed the backpack, unzipped the flap and reached inside. "Energy bar?"

"I'm glad I packed these for you. I'm starving." She tore off the wrapping. "Tell me about this backup."

So much for distracting her. He peered into the backpack. There were two bars left. Like his bullets, their food would have to be rationed. He looked up at the sunlight slanting through the opening above them. "We've probably got three more hours of daylight before we can make our move."

"Were those the federal marshals?"

He shrugged, hoping against hope that she'd drop the topic.

She took a bite of the energy bar and chewed. Her eyes were suspicious. "Are you going to tell me? Were those the feds or not?"

"I can't say for certain."

"Why not?" Her voice was sharp. "This is getting really annoying."

"I'm not lying to you," he said.

"Hard to believe, Jack. That one guy had a distinct accent. Did you hear his voice at the safe house or not?"

Evading her inquiries wouldn't be easy. She was smart and determined. His glance bounced off the rocky walls of their hiding place. Spending the next couple of hours in this enclosed space with Caitlyn slinging questions every few seconds would make him crazy. Might as well tell her the truth and get it over with.

"I can't remember," he said.

"Can't remember the names of the marshals? Or can't—"

"I don't remember much of anything." He moved away from her, returning to his position against the cavern wall. He felt as if he was literally stuck between a rock and a hard place. "When I got hit on the head, a lot of memories fell out."

"Seriously?" She scrambled around until she was beside him, facing him. Anger sparked in her eyes as she braced her hand against the wall beside his head and leaned in close for her interrogation. "Are you telling me that you have amnesia?"

"Something like that."

"Oh, please. If you don't want to tell me the truth, just say so. Don't insult me by making up a ridiculous excuse."

The irony irritated him. When she'd thought he was a handyman, she'd been more than willing to accept his lies. The truth was harder to swallow. "Believe what you want."

"If you have amnesia, how did you remember Mark Santoro?"

"I watched him die on the street in Chicago. A hell of a vivid memory." Through his shirt he felt the ragged edge of the scar on his belly. He'd been shot on that street. "I was never a soldier, but I understand chain of command. Mark Santoro was my captain. I was supposed to protect him, and I failed. That memory is never going to fade."

"What about the safe house?" she asked. "You remembered being at the safe house."

"I have a recollection of the place." He might even be able to locate the house again. There was a shake shingle roof, a long porch, a red barn. He shook his head. "The only thing I know for certain is that I need to be at the trial on Tuesday."

"Uh-huh."

"True story."

"This amnesia of yours," she said, "it comes and goes. Is that right? You remember whenever it's convenient?"

"I wish." He glared back at her. "If I knew who to call for backup, I'd have been on the phone first thing. Playing hide-and-seek with Rojas isn't my idea of fun."

She backed off, but only a few inches. Her expression remained skeptical as she chomped on her energy bar. "Head injuries can cause all kinds of strange problems. I just don't know whether to believe you."

"I don't give a damn if you trust me or not. There's only one thing that's important—for us to get out of this mess in one piece."

"Why did you tell me about the amnesia?"

"Because you're a pain in the butt." He held her by the shoulders and confronted her directly. "I don't want to spend the next couple of hours being interrogated."

She shoved at his chest. "Get your hands off me."

"Gladly."

He moved around her and picked up the tool belt. There were screwdrivers, a file and a rasp. "I don't suppose there's a knife in this belt. Or a nail gun."

Her voice was quiet but still persistent. "You told me about the wise old man in the desert who taught you about awareness. A memory?"

"I remember him. He trained me, but I don't know why." Without looking at her, he continued, "I'm aware of speaking Spanish, but don't know how I learned the language. I have skills. Seems like I'm a pretty good marksman."

"I'll say. Back at my cabin you made every bullet count."

Though he was pleased that she'd noticed his ability, he didn't let down his guard. "I don't know how I learned to handle a gun. I have no memory of being trained."

"When you said—"

"That's it, Caitlyn. I'm done talking."

His ability to remember was far less important than their immediate problem. They needed to get as far away from Rojas as possible. And they needed to move fast.

No MATTER HOW CAITLYN shifted around, she couldn't get comfortable. When she leaned against the wall of the cavern, her backbone rubbed painfully on the hard surface. Her butt was sore and cold from sitting on the damp rocks beside the water. With her knees pulled up, she wrapped her arms around her legs and watched Jack as he sorted through the various implements on her tool belt.

Who was this man? Reluctantly she decided to accept his explanation that he suffered from some form of amnesia. His head injury provided validation for that claim, and she was well aware of the unpredictability of trauma to the brain.

Okay, then. Amnesia.

The only identity that made sense was Tony Perez, member of the Santoro crime family who supposedly died on the streets of Chicago. As Perez, he'd be a witness—a protected witness—whose testimony could convict the elder Rojas brother.

But the searcher who poked around in the lower cave had mentioned a few things that didn't fit. Why would Tony Perez be able to call for backup? And what kind of jungle mission would he have been undertaking? She wished that she'd had more time on her computer to research his background.

Though Jack had made it very clear that he didn't want to answer questions, she wasn't the kind of passive woman who could simply sit back and take orders. She cleared her throat before speaking. "It seems to me that it might be extremely useful to know who you might call for backup."

He grunted in response.

"If you gave me a chance, I might be able to jog your memory. Maybe we could start with the last thing you remember and work backward."

He flipped a Phillips screwdriver in his hand and gripped the handle as if using it to stab. He stared at the tip and frowned. "I know you'd like a simple solution. So would I. But amnesia isn't like misplacing my keys or forgetting where I parked my car. There are empty spaces inside my head."

She didn't want to give up. "We could try. It wouldn't hurt."

"What if I don't like what I remember?" He flipped the screwdriver again. His hands were quick, his coordination excellent. "It might turn out that those blank spots are filled with nasty secrets."

"Are you saying that you'd rather not know?"

"I don't mind being Jack Dalton, a man with no past."

She understood that while he was working for Mark Santoro he might have done things he'd rather forget. But to throw away his entire history? "You're not a bad person. You have a conscience. You agreed to come forward and testify."

"I want Rojas to pay for the murder of Mark Santoro," he said.

"That's a starting place," she said, encouraging him to continue. "What else do you want?"

"To get you to safety."

He focused on her. In the dim light of the cavern, his features weren't clear. She felt rather than saw the heat emanating from him. He smoldered, and she felt herself melting. On a purely visceral level, it didn't matter where he came from or who he was. She knew, without doubt, that he was dedicated to rescuing her. Still, she persisted. "Your memories could help us. There might be someone you could call."

"Someone from the Santoro family?" The corner of his mouth lifted in a wry grin. "That might not be good news for you."

Probably not. The notorious crime family from Chicago wouldn't welcome a reporter into their midst. "Better them than Rojas."

"Leave my past alone, Caitlyn."

He returned his attention to the tool belt. She watched him as he evaluated each implement. In his hands, a paint scraper became a tool for slashing. The hammer was an obvious weapon, as was the crowbar. After discarding wrenches and small screwdrivers, he took the belt apart and reassembled it as a sort of holster.

She couldn't help asking another question. "Have you done this before?"

"Not that I remember. I seem to be good at improvising, using whatever comes to hand."

"Maybe you're MacGyver."

"Anything can be used as a weapon. A belt buckle or a shoelace. A mirror. A rock. It's all about intent."

"And what are your intentions?"

"To be prepared in case we're attacked. Frankly, I'm hoping I won't need a weapon. We'll get to your car and drive to a safe place where I can turn myself in to the authorities. How far are we from Denver?"

"About an hour. If we were going cross-country, we'd actually be closer to Colorado Springs."

He looked up at the sunlight that spilled through the opening in the rocks. "We still have a couple of hours before we can move. Might be smart to catch some shut-eye."

During the time she'd spent embedded with the troops, she'd learned to nap in difficult surroundings. She agreed that it was wise to be rested before they took on the final leg of their escape. "I don't think I can sleep."

Jack settled himself against the cavern wall and beckoned to her. "Lean against me. You'll be more comfortable."

Or not. Whenever she got close to him, her survival instincts were replaced by a surge of pure lust. Why did she have this crazy attraction to him? Sure, he was handsome, with that thick black hair and steamy green eyes. Definitely a manly man, he was her type. But she'd been around plenty of macho guys when she was with the troops. None of them affected her the way Jack did.

He noticed her hesitation. Again, he treated her to that sexy, wry grin. "Scared?"

"Of you?" Was her voice squeaking? "No way."

"Then come here. Use me for a pillow."

Pillows were soft and cuddly. Snuggling up against Jack's muscular body wouldn't be the least bit relaxing. She needed a different plan.

Reaching into her pocket, she took out her cell phone. "We could call the authorities in Denver right now."

"You know that phones can be tracked with a GPS signal."

"You said that before. I get it. But this is a secure phone. It was issued to me by my former employer. It's safe."

"Are you clear on that point?"

"Crystal."

He closed his eyes. "We wait until dark."

Chapter Nine

Jack always slept with one eye open. That wasn't a memory but a fact. Being a light sleeper was as indelible as being right-handed.

He leaned against the wall of the cavern. His body slipped into a state of relaxation, allowing his energy to replenish, but part of his mind stayed alert. Even when he was a kid, he knew it was important to be on guard so he would hear the staggering footsteps in the hallway outside the bedroom. His eyes were attuned to deal with the flash of light when that bedroom door crashed open. He knew the smell of the man who meant to hurt him—sweat and whiskey and hate.

Danger was ever present. Survival depended on being ready for the inevitable slap across the face or belt lashing. Or Rojas.

While sleeping, he remained aware of Caitlyn's movements. She tried curling up by herself at the edge of the water. Then she got another energy bar from the backpack. She stood and paced two steps in one direction then the other, like an animal in a cage that was too small. Finally, she settled beside him. Her head rested on his chest, and her slender body curved against him.

He pulled her close. The way she fit into his embrace gave him a sense of warmth and comfort that went beyond the sensual pleasure of holding a beautiful woman. Physically, they were well matched. And there was a deeper connection. Her unflagging curiosity drove him nuts, but he appreciated her intelligence, her wit and her stamina. When he'd given her the clear directive to run, she hadn't complained. Caitlyn wasn't a whiner. She'd been affected by her memories of war but hadn't been broken.

He'd been with other women, many others. One had been special, cherished and adored. He had loved before. Part of him longed to see his lover's face again and to hear her soft, sweet voice. But that was not to be. Without remembering the specifics, he knew his love was gone. Forever.

When Caitlyn moved away from him, he felt the empty space where her head should have been resting. His eyelids opened to slits. The sunlight filtering into the cavern had dimmed to grayish dusk.

He watched as Caitlyn climbed toward the ledge leading out of the cavern. "Where are you going?"

"I'll get better reception here. I need to call Heather at the Circle L Ranch and tell her where the horses are tethered."

"It's best if no one else gets involved. Don't tell her anything else."

"I understand." After she made the call, she looked down at her phone.

"I have a message from Danny. It came through about twenty minutes ago."

He stretched and yawned. The brief sleep had refreshed him enough to continue with his simple plan to get her car and drive to safety. He was aware of potential obstacles, especially since the federal marshals were involved. It might be useful to hear from the local deputy. "Go ahead and play back the message."

As she held the phone to her ear and listened, he watched her posture grow tense and angry. "You need to hear this."

She played back the message on speaker. Danny's voice was low. "Hey, Caitlyn. I found the owners of the gray mare. I thought I remembered seeing that horse."

Danny had stumbled across the safe house. *Bad news.*

The deputy continued, "The owner wants to thank you and maybe give you a reward. Let me tell you where the house is."

He gave directions, starting with "It's not far from where that Arapaho Indian guy lived. I think his name was Red Fire. Yeah, that's it. Red Fire. Turn off the main road at Clover Creek."

After he outlined a couple more twists and turns, he ended the call by saying, "I'll wait here until you arrive. Hurry."

Jack rose and crossed the cavern to stand beside her. Dusky light slid across her stricken face. She whispered, "Danny was warning me. When we were growing up, 'Red Fire' was our code for trouble."

"Even though he made the call, he was telling you to stay away."

"Rojas has him." Her voice quavered. "We can't leave him with that bastard."

The deputy's probability for survival was slim. Neither Rojas nor the feds could afford to release a lawman who would testify against them. Jack knew that the smart move was to drive away and try not to think about what was happening to Caitlyn's friend. It was more important for him to get to that trial and testify.

But Jack wasn't made that way. He couldn't leave someone else to die in his place. "Give me the phone."

"What are you going to do?"

"I'm going to save your friend."

He hit the callback button and waited. With each ring, Jack's hopes sank lower. Danny could already be dead.

The voice that finally answered was unfamiliar. "I'm expecting you."

"I'll be there." As soon as the words left his mouth, Jack knew that he'd done hostage negotiations before. The first step was to give the hostage takers what they wanted. Then demand proof of life. "I need to speak with Danny."

"He's tied up." The cryptic comment was followed by cold laughter. "All tied up."

"If I don't talk to him, you won't see me again. Not until we meet in court."

"Hold on." There were sounds of shuffling and a couple of thuds. Then Danny came on the phone. "It's me. Danny Laurence."

Jack asked, "Have you been harmed?"

"Where's Caitlyn?"

She spoke up. "I'm here, Danny. Are you all right?"

"I'm fine," he said. "The only way we're going to get through this is to do what they say."

Jack assumed that Rojas had threatened Danny's family and friends. He must have told Danny that if he caused trouble, his loved ones would suffer. "I can arrange protection for—"

"No." Danny was adamant. "The less they know, the better."

Jack agreed. He had a new respect for the deputy, who was willing to sacrifice himself to keep others safe.

The other voice came on the phone. "You'd be wise to listen to Danny. Contact no one else."

"Understood."

"Come to the house. You know where it is. And bring the girl."

To do as he said would be suicide. "I want a different meeting place. Neutral ground."

"You have no right to make demands."

"I'm the one you want," Jack said. "I assume I'm talking to Gregorio Rojas. Am I right?"

"Continue."

"If you don't get your hands on me, I'll testify at that trial in Chicago. And your brother will go to jail for the rest of his life. You want me. And the only way you'll get me is if you agree to a meet."

There was a long, very long, pause. "Where?"

"I'll call you back in fifteen minutes with the location. Bring Danny. If he's hurt, the deal is off."

Jack disconnected the call and turned off the phone. As he strapped on the tool belt that had been modified to a holster, he turned to Caitlyn. "How long will it take to get to your house?"

"If we move fast, fifteen minutes. What are we going to do?"

"I need for you to think of a meeting place for the hostage exchange. Somewhere secluded."

He climbed through the slit in the rocks and reached back to help her. The sun had dipped behind the mountains, and the forests were filled with shadow. Though Jack would have preferred waiting for at least an hour when it would be pitch-dark, he knew they didn't have that option. They needed to strike quickly. He started a mental clock, ticking down fifteen minutes until the next phone call.

Rojas had the advantage of superior manpower and weapons. Jack's edge was his mobility and his instincts. And Caitlyn. If Jack had been alone in the forest, he would have wasted precious moments figuring out where he was. She knew the way through the trees and back to her cabin. She leapt from rock to rock. In unobstructed stretches, they ran full out. They were at the long slope leading down to her house within ten minutes.

At the edge of the trees, he crouched beside her. "Good job."

She accepted his compliment with a nod. "I don't see any light from my cabin. Do you think Rojas left a man there?"

His henchmen weren't clever enough to leave the lights turned off. The federal marshals were another story. They'd know better than to betray their position by making themselves at home.

He figured that the marshals would want to distance themselves from the hostage situation as much as possible. They probably weren't at the safe house with Rojas, which left them free to search.

Thinking back to his time in custody, Jack remembered three marshals. Two of them, including the guy with the Texas twang, had been on horseback at the cave. Where was the third man? Hiding in Caitlyn's cabin? In the barn?

"How do we do this?" she asked.

"Give me the car keys."

"I'm driving," she said. "I know my way around this area and you don't. It's logical for me to be behind the wheel."

Logical, but not safe. He didn't want her to be part of the action, but leaving her alone and unguarded in the forest was equally dangerous. "What if you freeze up again?"

"I won't. Not while Danny's life is in danger. I know what's at stake."

There wasn't time to argue, and she was right about knowing the territory. "We'll slip down the hill, run to your car and get in. If we're fired upon, keep your head low and drive fast."

She nodded. "It's been fifteen minutes. You should call

them back. The best meeting place I can think of is the old cemetery by Sterling Creek. It's a half mile down a road that nobody ever uses."

"Don't need directions." He took out the phone. "They won't agree to our location anyway."

"How do you know?"

"Apparently, I've done stuff like this before. I'm sure that Rojas will want the advantage of choosing the location."

His phone call took less than a minute. As he predicted, Rojas refused to come to the cemetery and insisted that they use a deserted ranch house. Jack ended the call by saying, "That's too far from where we are. I'll get back to you in ten minutes."

"Wait," she said. "You need to tell them more. They'll hurt Danny."

"Not yet they won't." He shoved her phone into his pocket. "Follow me down the slope. If the third marshal is in your house, he might start shooting. That's your signal to run back to the cave and stay there."

"What about—"

"No more talking."

He started down the hill, keeping to the shadows as much as possible. A twig snapped under his boot. There was no way to muffle the sound of their footsteps. He compensated by moving swiftly. If they got to the car before the marshal had time to pinpoint their location and react, there was a good chance that they could get away clean.

He dove into the passenger seat. Caitlyn was behind the wheel of her dark green SUV. She cranked the key in the ignition and they drove away from her cabin.

No shots were fired. There was no sign of pursuit.

Instead of being relieved, Jack's suspicions were aroused. The marshals were up to something. He was damn sure that Rojas used a threat to Danny's family to get him to cooperate, and he was equally certain that the three traitorous marshals wouldn't allow a bloodbath. If the feds had any hope of protecting their butts, they had to turn the tide in their direction. They needed to look like heroes.

Jack expected the marshals to throw him under the bus.

In the meantime, he and Caitlyn had to get Danny away from Rojas. She was doing her best, driving like a Grand Prix master on the narrow, graded road.

"New car?" he asked. The interior still had the fresh-from-the-showroom smell.

"I'm leasing for a year." Her eyes riveted to the road ahead. "She handles well for a clunky SUV."

"She?"

"All my vehicles are female," she said. "This one is kind of sedate. I'm calling her Ms. Peacock because she's green."

He figured that Ms. Peacock had all the bells and whistles, including GPS mapping and a locator. She wasn't the best car to use for a getaway. "How long until we get to the safe house?"

"At normal speed, twenty minutes. I can do it in fifteen."

"Make it eight," he said.

She shot him a quick glance and juiced the accelerator. "You got it."

When he made the next phone call, his goal was to keep Rojas on the line for as long as possible while they made their approach. Timing was essential to the success of his plan.

Jack had no intention of meeting Rojas at an alternate location. He wanted to be in position for an attack when they were leaving the safe house and not expecting to see him.

After he and Rojas bickered back and forth, Jack said,

"I'll agree to a meeting at the place you named. It's going to take us forty-five minutes to get there, but Caitlyn knows where it is."

"Forty-five minutes, then."

"And I've got a couple of conditions," Jack said. "First of all, you can't harm Danny. I need your word of honor that you won't touch him."

"Done." Rojas was terse.

He was lying. Rojas had as much honor as a snake. Jack lied back to him. "I trust you, Gregorio. We can handle this hostage exchange without bloodshed. Here's how it's going to work."

Speaking slowly, Jack rambled through a complicated plan to trade himself for Danny, while Caitlyn careened around a wide curve. They passed the entry gate for the Circle L Ranch and a fenced meadow populated with a herd of cattle. The road narrowed slightly and went through a series of hairpin turns before opening up into a straight line. They were nearing the intersection with a main road.

He talked to Rojas about being set free on a plane to Costa Rica. "And you'll never hear from me again."

"Yes, yes. Whatever you want."

"Well, then. We have an agreement," Jack said. "I'll see you in about forty-five minutes."

He disconnected the call and turned to Caitlyn. "How far are we from the safe house?"

"Within a mile."

"Nice job, Speed Racer."

"You should see me in a Hummer."

This woman had been to war. She knew how to handle herself when she wasn't disabled by fear. "Cut your headlights. Get as close as you can without turning into the driveway."

She nodded. "What do we do when we get there?"

"You park the car and stay with it. I'll get close and grab Danny. We'll run back to you."

When she turned off the headlights, she had to slow her frantic speed; there wasn't enough daylight to see the road clearly. "What if something goes wrong?"

"It won't."

Not if he could help it.

Chapter Ten

After her mad race on the twisting gravel roads, Caitlyn was dizzy with emotion. Excited by the speed. Angry about Danny's capture. Grateful that she'd made it to the safe house without careening into a tree or spinning off a hairpin turn into a ditch. Apprehensive about what might happen next. Adrenaline surged through her veins. Her skin prickled with enough electricity to power a small village.

With fingers clenched on the steering wheel, she eased her green SUV into a hidden spot behind a stand of pine trees and killed the engine. Jack had told her to wait. She was unarmed; there was nothing she could do to help rescue Danny.

While embedded with the troops, she'd been in this position before. Watching as the soldiers prepared for a mission. Hearing the determination in their voices. Knowing that some of them would not come back.

But she wasn't an observer anymore. *This is my mission. My friend is in danger.* It would have been reassuring to have a combat helmet and ballistic vest to gird for warfare. Not that the clothing or the weaponry made a difference. Being battle-ready was a state of mind that came from training and experience that she didn't have. Though she'd been to war, she was a civilian.

If saving Danny had depended on writing a thought-provoking essay, Caitlyn would have been helpful. But in this situation? Jack knew better than she did.

She fidgeted in the driver's seat. From where she was parked, she couldn't even see the house. She needed to move. If she didn't take action, the tension building inside her would explode. After turning off the light that automatically came on when the door opened, she quietly unfastened the latch and crept from the vehicle. She approached the barbed-wire fence surrounding the property.

The waning moon hung low in the night sky, but there was enough starlight to see Jack as he darted through the tall brush toward the low, flat ranch house. He stayed parallel to the one-lane asphalt driveway that was roughly the length of a city block.

At the house, Rojas and his men made no attempt to conceal their presence. In addition to light pouring through the front and side windows, the porch was lit. To the right of the house was the horse barn and corral. The black SUV that had earlier visited her house was parked outside. And two other sedans, probably rentals. How many men were inside?

She paced along the fence line, then returned to her SUV, then back to the fence. Squinting hard, she saw Jack as he disappeared into the shadows near the house. He moved with stealth and confidence. In the natural order of things, she figured Jack was a predator. A dangerous man. The only reason he kept himself hidden was to surprise his prey.

But how could he possibly take on Rojas and his men with nothing more than a tool belt and two bullets? These men were killers, violent and sadistic. She'd read the news stories about the cartel crimes in Mexico. They were as brutal as the Afghani warlord she'd interviewed. Her mind flashed terrifying images. Memories. She had seen the mutilated corpses. *Stop! I can't go there. I can't let myself slip into fear.*

Amnesia would have been a relief. Jack was lucky to have his past erased, but she wouldn't have wished for the same fate. Not all her memories were bad; she'd had a happy childhood. There were many proud moments she never wanted to forget, like the first time she'd seen her byline in print and the thrill of tracking down a story. And Christmas morning. And her sixteenth birthday. And falling in love. Closing her eyes, she forced herself to remember a wonderful time.

Sunset on a beach. Palm trees swayed in the breeze. She held hands with a tall, handsome man as they walked at the water's edge. The cool water lapped at her bare ankles. She looked up at him and saw...

Jack! Shirtless and muscular, the scars on his torso were landmarks to the past he'd forgotten. His grin teased her as he leaned closer. Before they kissed, she opened her eyes.

The night surrounded her. She wanted Jack's embrace. To be honest, she wanted more intimacy than a simple kiss. If they got out of this alive, she would make love to him. Together, they'd create a memory—a moment of passion that was destined to never be repeated.

His destiny was set. After he testified, he'd disappear into the witness protection program. Even if that hadn't been the case, she really didn't see herself in a long-term relationship with a former member of the Santoro family.

She tucked a hank of hair behind her ear and stared toward the house. Why were they taking so long? They had to leave soon to get to the meeting place.

She wished Jack had explained what he was going to do, but she couldn't blame him for not outlining his plan. There hadn't been time to discuss options. And he really couldn't count on her for backup. Not after she'd frozen when fired upon. *That wouldn't happen again. It couldn't.*

Though she trembled, she felt no fear. Anger dominated her mind—white-hot anger. Tension set fire to her rage. She wanted to yell, not whimper.

Consciously, she fed the flame. She despised Rojas and his men, hated the way they victimized Danny and threatened his family. Their cruelty outraged her. She wanted justice and retribution for every criminal act the cartel had committed.

Her anger ran deep. There had been times—while she observed the troops—when she had wondered if she was capable of killing another human being. At this moment, she felt like she could.

The front door to the house opened, and she heard voices. A man stepped onto the porch. He was too far away for her to tell much about him, but she didn't think she'd seen him before. Had Rojas called in reinforcements?

From her vantage point outside the barbed wire, Caitlyn mentally took the measure of the distance between her SUV and the front door to the house. It was over a hundred yards, maybe closer to two hundred. Jack had told her to wait until he rescued Danny and they ran to the car. That plan wouldn't work if Danny wasn't capable of running.

She needed to bring her SUV closer.

FROM THE EDGE OF THE house, Jack watched a young man with a buzz cut saunter across the yard between the front door and the vehicles. His path led past the place where Jack was hiding, but Buzz Cut didn't notice him. This guy was oblivious. He flipped car keys into the air and caught them. His casual manner indicated that he wasn't a decision-maker but somebody who obeyed orders. Rojas must have sent Buzz Cut to bring the car around to the front door.

Using implements from the tool belt, Jack armed himself. The claw hammer was in his right hand. A screwdriver in the left. Though Buzz Cut carried a gun in a shoulder holster, Jack's weapons were also lethal. Not many men survived a hammer blow to the skull. Not that he intended to kill this guy. Not unless he had to.

A memory flashed in his brain.

Keeping a half-block distance, he tailed the man with fiery red hair. The bastard walked with his chest out and his arms swinging as though he was king of the world.

Pure hatred churned in Jack's gut. In his pocket his hand held a serrated-edge switchblade, illegal in this state. With one quick slash, he could sever the redheaded man's carotid artery. Within four minutes, the man would bleed out.

There were too many witnesses on the street. The timing wasn't right. Revenge would have to wait.

Jack shook his head to erase the memory. The past would have to wait; he needed to be one hundred percent focused on the present.

From quick glances through the windows of the house, he had counted seven men, including Rojas and the big guy named Drew, who was nursing his injured leg. He couldn't tell if any of these men were the federal marshals, but he didn't think so.

Danny was slumped over in a chair with his wrists tied to the arms. The black hood that covered his head counted as a positive sign. Rojas was making sure that the deputy wouldn't see too much.

Jack figured that Rojas and his crew would leave soon so they could get to the meeting place first and set up an ambush. They wouldn't be expecting an attack here. Since there were seven plus Danny, they'd need two cars.

When Buzz Cut pointed the automatic lock opener at the black SUV, Jack decided to make his first move. He could eliminate Buzz Cut and take his weapon without anyone being the wiser. Stepping out of the shadows, he sprinted toward the SUV.

By the time Buzz Cut realized that he wasn't alone and turned around, Jack was on top of him, looking into his eyes, seeing his disbelief and surprise. With the hammer tilted sideways, he swung carefully. The glancing blow was enough to knock Buzz Cut unconscious but not hard enough to shatter his skull. He'd live.

Grabbing the gun from the holster, he hauled the young man into the shadows beside the horse barn and returned to the black SUV. Jack slid behind the wheel and drove to the front door, where he left the engine running while he slid out the passenger-side door and waited on the opposite side of the car.

Two other men lumbered from the house. Both were stocky and muscular. They were gorillas, not the kind of guys you'd want to meet in a dark alley. Walking toward the other car—a dark sedan—they argued.

One of them was limping. He grabbed the other man's wrist and growled, "Give me the keys. I'll drive."

"You're injured. You should sit back and shut up."

"Don't tell me what to do."

The uninjured man shook off the other's grasp and took a couple of quick steps away from him.

Jack hoped these two would drive away before Rojas emerged from the house with Danny. If they left, he had two fewer adversaries to worry about.

"Hey!" The man with the limp rushed forward. The

effort of ignoring his pain showed in his clenched jaw. "I'm driving. You'll get lost."

"How can I get lost? We're supposed to follow the SUV."

That wasn't what Jack wanted to hear. With these two armed men in the car behind the SUV, he couldn't pull Danny away from his captors without getting both of them shot.

The threat from these two had to be eliminated, but quietly. If Jack fired a gun, he'd alert Rojas to his presence. That wouldn't be good for Danny.

It took a minimum exertion of stealth to approach the twosome as they fought over the car keys. They were so engrossed in their petty griping that Jack could have announced himself with a coronet fanfare and they wouldn't have noticed.

He aimed for the uninjured man first. A quick blow from the hammer took him down.

The second man reacted. He went for his gun. *Dumb move.*

Jack didn't think he'd been trained in martial arts, but he had experience in street fighting. Striking fast was key. While the other man reached for his gun, closed his fingers around the grip and drew the weapon, Jack made a single move—a backhanded slash with the screwdriver. The edge tore a deep gash. The gorilla gasped, looked down at the blood oozing from his gut. Jack finished him off with a roundhouse right to the jaw.

In a matter of seconds, both men lay unconscious at his feet. Jack took the car keys they'd been arguing about and threw them into the weeds.

Three down, four to go. One of the remaining men was Drew Kelso, the guy who would be slowed down by his leg injury. Another was Rojas who probably wasn't accustomed to doing his own dirty work. That left two armed thugs.

Jack holstered his hammer and screwdriver in the tool belt. His work as Mister Fix-it was over. For this portion of the rescue, he needed firepower. He gripped one of the semiautomatic handguns and ran toward the SUV that still had the engine running.

He resumed his position at the front of the SUV and crouched between the headlights. The bad thing about street fighting was that you couldn't plan ahead. Winning the fight was all about instinct and reaction. His only goal was to get Danny away from here unharmed.

Looking up the road, he tried to see where Caitlyn had parked her car. The outline was barely visible through a stand of trees. It wasn't going to be easy to get Danny all the way up that driveway, but he didn't want Caitlyn to come closer. He wanted her to stay safe, untouched. When he was done here, he wanted to be able to look into her clear blue eyes and assure her that the world wasn't a terrible place. Sometimes, the good guys came out on top.

The last group appeared in the doorway of the safe house. One man escorted Danny, holding his arm and shoving him forward. The black hood still covered Danny's head, and his wrists were handcuffed in front of him. He stumbled, and his escort yanked him upright.

Kelso and Rojas had not yet appeared.

Another man went to open the back door of the SUV.

Jack made his move. Using the butt of the gun, he smacked the guy holding Danny on the head. The guy staggered a step forward, leaning against the car. His legs folded.

"Danny," Jack whispered, "I'm on your side. Don't resist."

With one hand he yanked the hood off the deputy's head. With the other he pulled him out of the line of fire.

The guy who had been opening the car door grabbed for his holster. He was out of reach; Jack had to shoot. At this point-blank range, he'd blow a hole six inches wide in the guy's gut.

Though the automatic handgun was unfamiliar, Jack aimed for the thug's weapon and squeezed off a single shot. The thug's gun went flying. He screamed in pain and clutched his hand to his chest. Then he took off running.

Rojas and Kelso came onto the porch. They looked surprised by the chaos in the yard. These men weren't accustomed to being hunted. They considered themselves to be the attackers, the predators at the top of the food chain. Not this time.

Rojas stared into his face. "You. Nick Racine."

The name stopped him short. Echoes of memory surged inside him. An angry voice, his father, yelled the name. A woman whispered it in soft, sultry tones. A teacher took roll call. *Racine, Racine, Racine.*

"No." That wasn't him. He unleashed a spray of bullets toward the porch. Too late.

His few seconds of hesitation cost him dearly. It had been just enough time for Kelso and Rojas to retreat into the house.

Though Jack cursed himself for his lapse, he wasn't entirely sure that he would have shot them. It was his duty to take them into custody. Death was too easy for these bastards; they deserved a life sentence in a small, gray cell. *His duty?* What the hell was he thinking?

He pulled Danny around to the opposite side of the car. If he could maneuver them into the vehicle, he might be able to drive away. As he reached for the door handle, a burst of gunfire exploded from inside the house. Bullets pinged against the black SUV. A window shattered. Using this vehicle wasn't a good option. It was directly in the line of fire. There had to be another way.

He looked at Danny. His face was battered and swollen. His eyes seemed unfocused. When he leaned against the car, he slid to the ground. His cuffed hands fell into his lap.

"Danny, can you hear me?"

He nodded slowly.

"Do you think you can run?"

He raised his hand to wipe the blood from his split lip. "I'll do whatever it takes."

His fighting spirit was admirable. But was he physically capable of moving fast? If Jack was alone, he could have easily escaped, but he couldn't make a dash across the open meadow while dragging an injured man. Peering around the front end of the car, he returned fire. Should have killed Rojas and Kelso when he had the chance. Shouldn't have held back.

He and Danny were trapped, pinned down.

He turned his head and saw Caitlyn's green SUV zooming down the driveway. She was driving in reverse, coming to their rescue.

For once in his life, he wasn't alone. He had Caitlyn for a partner, and she was one hell of a good woman.

Chapter Eleven

Driving backward down a long driveway wasn't easy. Caitlyn slipped off the asphalt and heard the slap of brush against the side of her SUV. Her tires skittered on the loose gravel at the edge of the drive.

The bursts of gunfire rattled inside her brain, but she didn't succumb to a paralyzed PTSD flashback. When she'd been standing at the barbed-wire fence and had seen Jack and Danny pinned down by gunfire, she knew she had to rescue them. Nothing else mattered.

Looking over her shoulder, she saw the headlights of the black SUV. There was plenty of time to hit her brakes, but she decided to use Ms. Peacock as a battering ram, putting the other vehicle out of commission.

Her rear end smacked the front grille of the black SUV with a satisfying crash that jolted her back against the seat. Good thing she'd buckled up. Bullets snapped against her car. The rear windows splintered. Ducking low in her seat, she should have been terrified, but her focus was on the rescue. *Please, God, let them get away unharmed. Don't let anything happen to…*

The back door to her SUV swung open. Danny crawled inside. He'd been beaten. His face was red as raw meat. She'd never been so glad to see him.

"Caitlyn, I didn't mean for you to come after me. When

I gave you the 'Red Fire' signal, I thought you'd call the sheriff and—"

"Shut up, Danny."

Looking over her shoulder, she saw Jack take aim and blast the tires of the black SUV before he dove in beside Danny. As soon as his door closed, she slipped into Drive and took off. At the turn to the main road, the tail end of her SUV fishtailed, but she maintained control. Ms. Peacock was doing a fine job. Caitlyn might have to change her name to something less ladylike and more daring. Maybe she should be the Green Hornet.

Jack reached between the seats and rested his hand on her shoulder. His fingers tightened in a gentle squeeze. "Thanks."

"You told me not to move, but when I saw you and Danny trapped, I had to help you."

"You did exactly the right thing, babe."

Usually when a man called her "babe" or "honey" or "sweetheart," she snapped at him. "Babe" sounded sexy when Jack said it. "Where are we going?"

From the backseat, Danny said, "Circle L. We were supposed to go there for dinner, Sandra and me. I've got to make sure she's okay. And Heather, too."

"It's going to be okay," Jack said calmly. "Let's see if we can get those cuffs off."

"Not important." Danny's voice was hoarse with urgency. "I have to see them. You don't understand."

"Sure, I do," Jack said. "Rojas threatened you. He told you that your wife and sister would be harmed if you didn't cooperate. Is that right?"

"Yes."

"I expect that he went into brutal details because that's the kind of man he is. Sadistic bastard." Though Jack kept his tone low and controlled, she heard the steely echo of his anger. "Those look like they might be your own cuffs. Got a key?"

"There's an extra key in my wallet. Back pocket."

Keeping her eyes on the road, Caitlyn said, "We can telephone Heather if you want."

"Good idea," Jack said. "We won't be bothered by Rojas for a little while. His big, black SUV isn't going anywhere. Why don't you pull over, Caitlyn. You can take care of Danny, and I'll drive."

She guided the car to a stop on the shoulder. When she turned in her seat, she saw that Jack had removed the tool belt and was unlocking Danny's cuffs. She took out her cell phone and hit the speed dial for the Circle L Ranch. Heather answered in a brisk, no-nonsense tone.

"It's Caitlyn. Are you all right?"

"Sure am."

"And Sandra? Is she there?"

"I'm fine. Sandra's fine. I picked up your tethered horses, and they're fine." Her voice dropped. "What's going on? What kind of trouble have you gotten yourself into?"

Caitlyn was satisfied. If Heather had been in danger, she would have found a way to tell her. "There's somebody here who wants to talk to you."

She passed the phone to Danny. His hand was shaking so much that he could barely hold it. "I love you, sis. I don't tell you enough. But I do." He gasped out a sob. "Put my wife on the phone."

Giving Danny some privacy, Caitlyn left the car and circled around to the back. She winced as she observed the amount of damage she'd done. One fender and the tail-light were smashed. The rear door to her SUV was beyond repair. Three windows were broken, and there were bullet holes along the driver's side. Explaining this incident to her insurance company wasn't going to be easy.

Jack stepped around the other side of the car and stood facing her. His hand slid down her arm in a caress, and he took the car keys from her. "If anything happens to me, there's something I want you to know."

"What do you mean?" As far as she was concerned, they were out of danger. Almost. "Nothing is going to happen to you."

His mouth curved in that teasing grin that made her want to kiss him. "Just in case."

"Damn it, Jack. Do you always have to look on the dark side?"

"Like I told you before, I always plan for the worst."

Reaching up, she stroked the rough stubble on his jaw. The light from the waning moon and the stars outlined the rugged planes of his face. "I couldn't tell exactly what you did at the safe house, but from what I saw, you were amazing. You caused enough concussions to keep a brain specialist busy for weeks."

"Assuming those guys had functional brains."

One thing she had observed didn't make sense. "It looked like you had the drop on Rojas. But you didn't shoot."

"Not my job," he said.

As far as she knew, he'd been an enforcer for the Santoro family. In that line of work, she was fairly sure that his duties included murder. When she thought about it, she realized that Jack hadn't killed anyone. Not at the safe house. Not at her cabin. "I'd like to know more about this job of yours."

"So would I." He tapped the side of his head. "Amnesia."

"Convenient."

"Not really."

His large hand slipped around her neck, and he pulled her closer. His lips were warm against hers. As she leaned toward him, the tips of her breasts grazed his chest. A shiver of awareness washed through her, leaving a tingling sensation.

When they kissed, she was hungry for more. Especially now. She knew her time with Jack was limited. Her torso pressed firmly against him. Her arms encircled him.

"Caitlyn," Danny bellowed from inside the car.

She tore herself away from Jack's embrace. As guilty as a teenager caught in the act, she put a polite distance between them. "I guess we have places to go."

"Here's what I want you to know," he said. "You're going to be all right."

Why was he telling her this? She cocked her head to one side. "Explain."

"You have doubts about yourself and your career. That's why you're living in the mountains like a hermit."

Though his characterization irked her, she didn't deny it. "Go on."

"You're scared. But you don't have to be. You're tough, Caitlyn. You're strong enough to take whatever life throws at you. If we had more time together, I'd—"

"Caitlyn," Danny called again. "We need to get going."

Jack shrugged. "I believe in you. Whatever happens, you're going to be fine."

As he walked past her on his way to the driver's seat, he patted her butt. Again, this wasn't a gesture she would usually accept without complaint, but she said nothing.

His reassurance was shockingly perceptive. It didn't seem fair that a man who was so good-looking and capable would also be wise.

In spite of the time she'd spent alone—time that was supposed to be for reflection and renewal—she hadn't made the connection between her PTSD fear and her doubts about her career. She'd been afraid of just about everything. Until now.

When she'd realized that Jack and Danny needed her, she'd been able to overcome her fear and do what had to be done. *I'm going to be all right.*

She was damaged but not broken. Her life would mend. All the energy she'd poured into fixing up the cabin could be turned into something she was actually good at.

In her heart, she'd always known what she was meant to do. She was a journalist, a seeker of truth. Losing her assignment in the Middle East didn't negate her skill or her talent. There were plenty of other stories to write…starting with Jack. He had a story she was itching to write.

As she settled into the backseat next to Danny, she asked Jack, "Do you need directions to the Circle L?"

"I remember the way."

Of course he would. He did everything well. When she turned her attention to Danny, her mood darkened. She was accustomed to seeing her old friend as a cool, confident leader—the most popular guy in the county, the local hero. Being held hostage had devastated him, and she feared that these wounds went deeper than the bruises on his face. His shoulders slumped. His uniform was stained with blood, torn and disheveled. The acrid smell of sweat clung to him.

Gently, she took his hand. Instead of offering false reassurances, she said the only positive thing she could think of. "We're almost at the Circle L. You'll be with your wife soon."

"I called the sheriff," he said. "He'll arrange for bodyguards for Sandra and Heather until that sick bastard is in custody."

From the front seat, Jack said, "Arresting Rojas will be dangerous."

"You don't have to tell me." With an effort, Danny lifted his head and looked toward the front seat. "You're the man they're looking for, aren't you? The witness."

"That's right," Caitlyn informed him. "He's also the guy who saved your butt."

"And I thank you for that," Danny said. "I didn't think I'd get away in one piece. Thought I was a dead man."

She didn't like seeing him this way. She missed his natural arrogance. "I wish there was something I could do for you. I don't have any first-aid stuff in the car."

"It's all right." He exhaled slowly and spoke to the back of Jack's head. "You did a good job negotiating. I only heard one side, but you convinced them to do what you wanted."

"I had an advantage," Jack said. "I knew Rojas would lie. He'd try to set up a meet where he could get there first and set up an ambush. I just had to stall him long enough so that I could beat him to the punch."

"What's your name?" Danny asked.

Caitlyn answered, "You can call him Jack."

"As in Jack Dalton?" Danny turned toward her. "I thought we established that Jack Dalton was in jail sleeping off a drunk and disorderly."

There was no simple way to explain how she'd gotten involved with Jack and how he had amnesia. "Just call him Jack for now."

Danny sank back against the seat and closed his eyes. His lips barely moved as he spoke. "You were always good at getting yourself into trouble, Caitlyn. Remember? And you thought you were so smart. A regular Little Miss Know-It-All."

"I don't just think I'm smart," she said. "I really am."

"Not always."

He seemed to be implying that she'd made a mistake. "Is there something you need to tell me?"

He spoke in a barely audible whisper. "How well do you know Jack?"

"Well enough to trust him with my life. Why do you ask?"

"There were eight men at the house, not including me. One of them was a federal marshal. He was dead." Danny looked down at his hands. "I knew he was a lawman because they pinned his badge to his forehead. He was… mutilated."

She glanced toward the front seat. Jack had worried about the whereabouts of the third marshal. Apparently, he wasn't in on the scheme with Rojas and the other two. And he had paid the ultimate price. "I'm sorry."

"How about you, Jack?" Danny's tone turned hostile. "Are you sorry about the marshal's death?"

"Stop it, Danny." What was wrong with him? She reached forward and tapped Jack on the shoulder. "We're here. This is the turn for the Circle L."

He drove through the open gate toward a well-lit, two-story ranch house that was painted white with slate-gray trim. A tall, thick cottonwood tree stood as high as the roof. Though there were no children at the Circle L, a tire swing hung from one of the branches.

The ranch looked like a peaceful sanctuary, but Caitlyn had the sense that something wasn't right. "Danny, what's going on?"

"There are my girls." The hint of a smile touched his lips as he gazed toward the wraparound porch where Heather stood with her arms braced against the railing. Beside her was a delicate-looking blonde who had to be Sandra. "They're safe. That's all that matters."

Jack pulled up close to the porch and parked. As soon

as he turned off the engine, two men emerged from the shadows. They moved quickly and with purpose, flanking the vehicle. The one who stood at the driver's side window pointed a rifle at Jack's head.

"U.S. marshal," he said with an unmistakably Texan twang. "I'm taking you into custody."

Chapter Twelve

If the marshals got their way, Jack would be cuffed and carted off, never to be seen again. Caitlyn refused to let that happen.

Her experience as a reporter in the world's hot spots had taught her to talk her way around just about anything. She'd been the first journalist to wrangle an interview with an aging Afghani warlord who fought with the mujahideen. She'd interviewed politicians and generals, even faced a serial killer on death row. Argument was her battlefield. Words were her weapons.

She bolted from the car and launched her verbal attack at the two marshals. Though she spoke with authority, she wasn't sure exactly what she'd said—something along the lines of legal and jurisdictional issues. "Danny was first deputy on the scene, which means he has custody. The Douglas County sheriff is responsible for this man."

Still holding his rifle on Jack, the Texan drawled, "What in hell are you yapping about?"

"He's ours," she said.

Brandishing the handcuffs she'd removed from Danny's wrists only moments ago, she opened the driver-side door and leaned inside. She whispered, "Let me handle this."

Staring straight ahead, Jack sat with both hands gripping the steering wheel. He turned his head and met her gaze. A bond of trust stretched between them. He believed in her; he'd told her so. It was time for her to justify his confidence.

As she snapped a cuff on his right wrist, he muttered under his breath, "You'd better be right about this."

"You should know by now. I'm almost always right."

"Little Miss Know-It-All."

When he stepped out of the car, she fastened the other cuff. Though she considered pressing the key into his palm so he could escape, she decided against it. Jack unchained was a force of nature, and she preferred a little finesse. The fewer bodies he left in his wake, the better.

Whirling, she faced the marshal from Texas. "Lower your weapon."

Danny—the big, fat traitor—was out of the car and appeared to be gathering his strength to object, but his wife, Heather and a couple of ranch hands swarmed around him, determined to help him whether or not he wanted to be helped.

One of the ranch hands bumped the rifle, and Heather snapped at the marshal, "You heard Caitlyn. Put down your weapon before you accidentally shoot yourself in the foot."

The Texan scowled but did as she said. His partner stalked around to their side of the car and spoke up. "Thanks for your help, folks. We've got it. This man is in our custody."

"Where's your warrant?" Caitlyn demanded.

"Don't need one." The gray-haired marshal produced his wallet and showed her his five-point star badge and his marshal credentials.

Caitlyn inspected his documents. "You're Marshal Steven Patterson."

"Correct." His jaw was speckled with bristly white

stubble, and his gray eyes were red-rimmed with exhaustion. "I'd appreciate if you'd step aside and let us do our job."

"Is this man a criminal?"

"No."

"Then why are you taking him?"

"He's a witness," Patterson said.

"A protected witness?"

"Correct."

"Pointing a rifle in his face doesn't seem like the best way to keep your witness safe," she said. "Maybe he doesn't want your so-called protection."

"He's in our custody. That's all you need to know."

Caitlyn nudged Heather's arm. "Does that sound right to you?"

Heather drew herself up to her full height. In her boots, she was nearly as tall as Jack, and she towered over Patterson. She hooked her thumb in her belt, right next to her revolver.

Caitlyn noticed that all the ranch hands were armed; they must have heard that there was danger, and they all watched Heather for their cues. She said, "Nobody does anything until my brother is taken care of. Sandra, you get Danny inside and call the doc."

Danny's petite blonde wife didn't need instruction; she was focused one hundred percent on her husband. Her devotion touched Caitlyn, and she would have been happy that Danny had found the perfect mate if she hadn't wanted to kill him for leading them into this trap.

Patterson spoke to Heather, "Looks like you have everything under control, ma'am. We'll be going now."

"Hold on," she said. "The Circle L is *my* ranch. *My* property. We do things *my* way. On *my* schedule."

"What are you saying?"

"I want you to answer Caitlyn's questions," Heather said.

"I don't answer to you." Patterson's polite veneer was worn thin. "I'm a federal officer, and your ranch isn't some kind of sovereign nation."

He couldn't have picked a worse argument, and Caitlyn was glad to see him digging his own grave. In this part of the world, respect for ownership of the land was as deeply engrained as the brands on the cattle. "Marshal Patterson, I can tell that you haven't spent much time in the West." To his partner, she said, "Explain it to him, Tex. Tell him how we feel about our land."

"The name's Bryant," said the younger marshal. "And I promise you, Miss Heather, we ain't here to cause trouble."

"I'll be the judge of that." Heather watched Sandra and the ranch hands escort her brother into the house, then she swung back toward Caitlyn. "What were you saying?"

"According to Marshal Patterson, he can take a witness into custody whether he wants to be protected or not. Now, that doesn't seem fair, especially since Patterson is a U.S. Marshal. The *U* and the *S* stand for *us,* as in you and me. He works for us. And I'm pretty sure I wouldn't want to be dragged off without my permission."

"She's got a point," Heather said.

"And I've got a job," Patterson said.

Caitlyn pulled out her cell phone. "Before you proceed, I need to make sure I have the facts right. I want to verify with the director of the Marshals Service or the attorney general."

"You can't."

"Oh, I think I can. I'm a journalist for a national news service." A little white lie since she wasn't actually employed at the moment. Using her cell, she snapped a photo of Patterson and his partner. "As a reporter, it's my job to raise holy hell if this situation isn't handled properly. Will you call the director? Or should I?"

Bryant asked his partner, "Can she do that?"

"Damn right I can."

Jack spoke up. "I'd advise you to listen to her."

"Why's that?"

"She might look like a Barbie doll, but this woman is G.I. Jane. She was embedded with the troops. Just came back from a war zone."

Patterson regarded her with a little more respect and a lot more loathing. "Is that so?"

"She knows people," Jack said. "Important people. The kind of people who could end the careers of a couple of marshals who screwed up."

"Bad luck for you," she said to Patterson. "I'm guessing that you're close to retirement. It would be a shame to lose your pension."

Two police vehicles careened down the driveway and parked, effectively blocking the exit. Four deputies rushed toward them, firing questions about what had happened to Danny and who was responsible. The confusion rose to the edge of chaos.

"Enough," Patterson said loudly. "All of you. Back off."

Frustration turned his complexion an unhealthy shade of brick red. He grasped Jack's upper arm—a move that Caitlyn saw as a huge mistake. The muscles in Jack's shoulders bunched as though he was preparing to throw off Patterson's hand. Even unarmed and in cuffs, he was capable of annihilating the two marshals. He might even be able to defeat the deputies, grab a vehicle and run.

But she didn't like the odds. There were too many guns. Too many nervous trigger fingers.

"Marshal Patterson," she said, "I have a suggestion."

He was desperate enough to listen. "Go on."

"You and your partner could step into the house. I'm sure Heather would let you use her office. And you could contact your superior officer for further instructions. When you produce verification that you have jurisdictional custody of this witness, we'll all be satisfied."

"Fine," he said, "but we're taking this man with us into the den while we make our phone calls."

It wasn't exactly the outcome Caitlyn had hoped for. The marshals weren't going to give up easily, and she'd have to come up with another ruse to get Jack away from them. But she'd bought some time. And nobody had gotten killed.

EVER SINCE DANNY MENTIONED the marshal who had been murdered and mutilated, Jack had been remembering details of what had happened to him at the safe house when Rojas came after him. How many times had he asked himself about the third marshal? At a deep, subconscious level, he had sensed the importance of the third man.

His name, Jack clearly remembered, was Hank Perry. His age, forty-two. He stood five feet ten inches. Brown hair and eyes. He was divorced, and his oldest son had just graduated from high school.

Hank Perry was dead. He'd given his life to protect Jack. Somehow, Jack would make sure that Perry's ultimate sacrifice would not be in vain. Somehow, he had to escape and make it back to Chicago for the trial.

Sitting on the floor in the den, he rested his back against a wall of bookshelves with his cuffed wrists in his lap. No doubt the two marshals in the room with him would have liked to hogtie him and pull a hood over his head, but they had to treat him humanely or Caitlyn would raise a stink.

Though he kept his face expressionless, Jack smiled inside when he thought of how she'd leapt to his defense. In spite of her dirty clothes and tangled blond hair, she'd transformed into a person of stature. With gravitas equal to Lady Justice herself, Caitlyn had created a wall of obstacles. Using wild-eyed logic and aggressive questions, she'd backed the marshals into a corner.

With grim satisfaction, he was glad that he'd taken a moment before they got to the ranch to tell her how he felt about her. Life experience had shaken her determination, but she'd made a full recovery. They made a good team. With her mouth and his muscle, they could have done great things together.

He looked over at Patterson, who slouched in the swivel chair behind the desk. He'd been on his cell phone for the past fifteen minutes. His side of the conversation was a lame explanation of how he and Bryant had been attacked, lost their witness and had their colleague murdered by Rojas.

Patterson admitted, over and over, that they'd made a mistake in not calling for backup. His excuse was that he feared a showdown with Rojas would give the cartel gang a reason to commit wholesale murder in this peaceful Colorado mountain community.

While he talked on his phone, Patterson juggled the SIG Sauer P-226 that he'd confiscated along with all the other weapons Jack had taken from Rojas. The SIG had belonged to Perry. Watching Patterson play with that honorable man's gun made Jack's blood boil.

The tall Texan marshal with the hundred-mile stare sauntered across the den and stood in front of Jack. With the toe of his cowboy boot, he nudged Jack's foot. "You're kind of quiet."

Brilliant observation, genius. Since they'd entered the den, Jack hadn't said a word. He'd been too consumed with memories of the midnight assault on the safe house. His mind echoed with the blast of semiautomatic gunfire and Perry's shout of warning. In the dark, he hadn't been able to identify the men who came after them. And he couldn't exactly recall how he'd gotten his head wound. But he'd seen Perry take a bullet and stagger back to his feet. With his last breath, he'd fought.

All of Patterson's talk about "doing his job" turned Jack's stomach. Patterson didn't have a clue about the real responsibility of being a U.S. marshal. He was a coward. A traitor.

Bryant squatted down to Jack's level. "We didn't get much chance to talk when you were at the safe house. I'm low man on the totem pole, so my assignment was to patrol outdoors."

Except for when Rojas showed up. Jack didn't remember seeing Patterson or Bryant during the attack. Their plan had probably been to leave him alone and unguarded.

Bryant continued, "Is all the stuff they say about you true? About the legendary Nick Racine?"

There was that name again. Racine, Nick Racine. Rojas had shouted it out, distracting him. If that was his real name, he ought to remember, but he couldn't make the connection. "What have you heard?"

"That you killed twelve men using nothing more than your belt buckle and your bare hands."

Though Jack was sure that hadn't happened, he nodded. If he impressed Bryant, he might convince the young man to take his side against Patterson. "What else?"

"You survived for a month in the desert with no food or water."

That was legendary, all right. "I had a good teacher, a wise old man who lived in Arizona. I owe it to him to pass on this knowledge. You could learn."

"Me?" Bryant shook his head. "I've never exactly been at the top of the class."

"It's not book learning. It's instinct."

"I got instincts." His brow lowered as he concentrated. "Seems like a damn shame to kill you, but we can't have you telling the truth to the Marshals Service."

In a low voice, Jack said, "It wasn't your fault. You were just following orders. It was Patterson who told Rojas the location of the safe house, wasn't it?"

"That's right. The old man arranged for the money, told me all we had to do was leave the house for an hour. Rojas was supposed to swoop in, grab you and take off. Slick and easy."

"Except for Perry," Jack said.

"Oh man, that was a big mistake. Rojas promised that Perry wasn't going to get hurt."

Yeah, sure, and then the Easter Bunny would leave them all pretty-colored eggs. Bryant was young, but he wasn't naive enough to trust a man like Rojas. At some point, the marshal had made a deliberate decision to turn his head and look the other way. "What was supposed to happen to me?"

"Guess I didn't think that far ahead."

Thinking wasn't Bryant's strong suit. "You can make up for your mistake. I'll take care of it."

"You're trying to trick me. That's part of the legend, too. You can change your identity like a shape-shifter."

"I'm not lying."

"I still don't believe you. The way Patterson tells it,

you've gone rogue. You know what that means? Being a rogue?"

Jack said nothing. The question was too ridiculous to answer. Though Bryant was a moron, he knew enough to follow orders from Patterson. A dangerous combination—stupidity and loyalty.

"One time," Bryant said, "I saw a television show about rogue elephants in Africa. My gal likes to watch that educational stuff. Anyway, there was this big, old elephant with giant tusks. We got a forty-six-inch flatscreen, and I'm telling you, that elephant was big. You might even say he was legendary. Like you."

"I'm an elephant?"

"A rogue," Bryant said. "The safari guy said the only way to handle a rogue was to kill him before he killed you."

I'm a dead man.

Chapter Thirteen

In the front room of the ranch house, Caitlyn positioned herself so she could keep an eye on the closed door to the den. Her mind raced as she tried to come up with a plan. Though she wanted to believe that the marshals wouldn't dare hurt Jack while he was in their custody, she knew better. They couldn't let him live. He had witnessed their treachery.

She could insist on accompanying them while they took Jack, but that might mean they'd kill her, too.

Looking down at the cell phone in her hand, she willed it to ring. She'd left a message for her former lover in Chicago, but she hadn't talked to him in years and didn't know if he was still employed at the newspaper. Her stateside contacts had dried up after she'd been stationed in the Middle East for so long. The only highly placed individuals she could call for a favor were in the military, and they couldn't help with this problem. If Patterson got the go-ahead from his superior officer, there wasn't much she could do to stop him from taking Jack.

When Heather handed her a steaming mug of coffee, Caitlyn grinned at her friend and said, "Thanks for taking my side."

"I didn't like those marshals when they showed up here and said they were supposed to protect us. Everybody who works at the Circle L has at least one gun. We take care of ourselves."

Considering the viciousness of Rojas and his men, Caitlyn was glad it hadn't come to a showdown. "Your instincts are right about the marshals. They're working with the bad guys."

"Fill me in."

Caitlyn glanced around at the other people in the room—ranch hands and a couple of deputies who were making phone calls. Since she didn't want to broadcast her story, she spoke in a quiet tone. "Jack is a federal witness who's supposed to testify on Tuesday in Chicago. He was in protective custody at a safe house that was attacked last night. He escaped, riding the gray mare that showed up on my doorstep. Here's the important thing, those marshals were supposed to be guarding him, but they stepped aside and let the bad guys go after him."

"Not all of them." Danny limped into the room, leaning on his pretty little wife for support. "One of the marshals died a heroic death in the line of duty."

Though he'd changed into a fresh shirt and his face was cleaned up, he still looked like hell. Caitlyn didn't feel sorry for him; Danny had betrayed them. "You knew the marshals were waiting here for Jack."

"They came here to protect my family."

"How did they know?" she demanded. "If they weren't working with Rojas, how did they know your family was in danger?"

"They were keeping an eye on the safe house," Danny said, defending them. "They must have seen what happened to me."

"And yet, they did nothing to rescue you. They didn't contact the sheriff, didn't call for backup. What kind of lawmen operate like that?"

"If they'd called for an assault on the safe house, I'd be dead right now."

His wife shuddered. "Don't say that."

"I'm okay, Sandra." He patted her arm. "There's nothing to worry about."

"You should be resting until the doc gets here. Let me take you upstairs to bed."

"Not until this is settled."

Her lips pulled into a tight, disapproving line, but she said nothing else. Caitlyn sympathized with her dilemma. It wasn't easy to love a stubborn man who wouldn't let anyone fight his battles for him. A man like Jack? Though she couldn't compare her relationship with Jack to a marriage or even to being in love, she cared about him. How could she not care? He'd saved her life. She thought of how he'd rescued her when she froze and his quiet heroics when at the safe house. He was a one-man strike force. But that wasn't why she cared so much. He'd seen inside her. He brought out the best in her. And, oh my, the man knew how to kiss.

She glared at Danny. "You don't know the whole story, but I'm not saying another word until you sit down. You look like you're about to collapse."

"She's right." Sandra gave her a grateful nod. "Let's all get settled and figure this out."

While Sandra made her husband comfortable in a leather armchair near the fireplace, Caitlyn perched on the edge of a rocking chair beside him. In as calm a tone as she could manage, she said, "You've got to admit that the actions of those two marshals were questionable. They had a whole day to track down Rojas and his men. What the hell were they doing?"

"Their job," Danny said. "They were tracking down their runaway witness."

At the cave, they'd come close. "They almost found us."

"Hold on." Heather held up her hand, signaling a halt. "It sounds like you and Jack were hiding from the marshals. Why would you do that?"

"We were on the run." When Caitlyn thought back, the afternoon seemed like a lifetime ago. "Rojas and his men showed up at my cabin. Because the gray horse came to my place, they must have figured that Jack had also been there. When they showed up, I was in the barn. They had guns. They were yelling. I've never been so scared in my life."

A residual wave of fear washed through her as she remembered turning to stone. "Jack had been watching my house. He rescued me. We took off on horseback."

"It's a damn good thing he was there," Heather said, "or else you'd be as beat up as my brother."

"We were hiding in that cavern that's not far from my cabin—the one with the water that runs all the way through it. Those two marshals nearly found us. I didn't see them, but I recognized the Texas accent."

"What did they say?" Heather asked.

She was tempted to lie and tell them that the marshals talked about murdering her and Jack, but she needed to stay on the high road. "Nothing incriminating."

"You should have spoken up," Danny said. "If you'd turned Jack in, this whole thing would have been over."

"Why are you so dead set against him?" Her anger flared. "He's a good man."

"He's a witness in a mob crime, probably a criminal himself who agreed to testify in exchange for immunity. I said it before, Caitlyn, and I'll say it again. You don't know anything about this guy."

Unable to sit still, she rose from the rocking chair so

quickly that it almost overturned. "I haven't finished telling what happened. If you don't mind, I'd like to continue."

"Go right ahead."

"While Jack and I were hiding, we got a message from Danny that told us he'd been captured by Rojas and was being held at the safe house. Jack didn't hesitate. Not for one minute. He knew he had to get Danny out of there."

Sandra's eyes widened. "Jack saved Danny?"

"If it weren't for Jack, you'd be a dead man. Right, Danny?"

He nodded slowly. "Right."

"I don't understand," Sandra said. "This man risked his life for you, and you're willing to sit back and watch while he gets dragged off in handcuffs."

"You're not seeing the big picture," he said.

"What's bigger than saving your life? Oh, Danny, you're not thinking straight."

He shifted in the big leather chair. "As far as I'm concerned, Jack could be working with Rojas. He might be responsible for the death of that marshal."

Caitlyn scoffed. "That's crazy."

"Yeah? Well, explain this for me. Jack had the drop on Rojas and that other guy. He could have pulled the trigger and taken them out. Why didn't he shoot?"

She didn't have a logical response. "I don't know."

"Because he's part of this scheme," Danny said. "He let Rojas get away. On purpose."

"Or maybe Jack isn't a murderer. Maybe he didn't want to shoot a man in the back."

"I'm sure he's got a smooth-talking answer," Danny said. "He's slick enough to convince you that he's some kind of hero, but I don't believe him. I'll take the word of a federal marshal over that of a criminal turned witness."

"Even when he saved you," Heather said, as she rose

from her chair and stood beside Caitlyn. "I hate to say this because you're my brother, but Danny, you're a jerk. And just about as perceptive as a fence post."

He frowned and looked toward his wife.

Sandra arched an eyebrow. "I'm with Heather on this. Caitlyn, what do you need?"

She was glad for these two votes of confidence. Before this was over, she'd need all the allies she could get. "I don't object to Jack being taken into protective custody. He wants to testify and break up the Rojas cartel. It's important to him. But I don't want those two marshals to be alone with him. They can't be trusted."

The front door swung open and Bob Woodley marched inside. He wasn't even pretending to be a docile, law-abiding citizen. In his right hand, he held his hunting rifle. In spite of his age, he emanated vitality and energy. His clothes were as disheveled as if he'd just gotten out of bed. His thick, white hair looked like he'd combed it with an eggbeater. As soon as he spotted Caitlyn, he charged toward her and pulled her into a bone-crunching hug.

"I'm sorry," he said. "I brought those bastards to your house. I put you in danger."

"You didn't know," she said.

"If anything had happened to you, I'd never forgive myself. Your mother would never forgive me."

"I'm fine." She separated from his ferocious hug and smiled up at him. "How did you hear about what happened?"

"Being an elected official, I have an inside track. Half the lawmen in Colorado—state patrol, SWAT teams, cops and deputies—are involved in a manhunt, looking for Rojas. I assume he's the fellow who told me his name was Reynolds."

"He lied to you, lied to everybody."

Danny struggled to get out of his chair. "Everybody else is mobilized. I should—"

"Sit down," Sandra said. "You've done enough."

Woodley took a look at him. "What the hell happened to your face?"

"Long story," he said. "Tell me what else is going on."

"I don't know much. As soon as I heard Caitlyn was in trouble, I jumped in my Ford Fairlane and raced over here." He turned back to her. "You're not hurt, are you?"

"I'm worried. Something terrible is about to happen, and I can't stop it."

Woodley drew himself up. "Tell me how I can help."

"That goes for me, too," Heather said. "I don't want to see the man who saved my brother's life get into any more trouble."

"All of you," Danny said, "stop it. You need to back off and let the marshals do their job. That's the law."

Caitlyn confronted him. "Sometimes, the law isn't right. Jack saved you. The marshals were willing to let you die."

"But I'm an officer of the law."

"That means you're sworn to enforce justice," she said, "even if it means stepping outside the law."

He winced. The bruises on his face were a crude reminder of what he'd suffered at the hands of Rojas. His gaze rested on his sister, then on his wife. "I wanted to keep you both safe."

"I know," Sandra said. She rested her small hand gently on his cheek. "Now, we have to do the right thing."

When they looked to her for direction, Caitlyn felt warm inside. Her heart expanded. These people were her friends, as loyal to her as the troops in combat.

The beginnings of a plan tickled the inside of her head. "There might be something we can do."

NEGOTIATING WITH BRYANT or Patterson was futile. Jack's only option was to fight. He had the vague outline of a plan. He'd wait until they left the Circle L Ranch; no point in having anyone else hurt in the crossfire. He'd go after Bryant first. Though the younger marshal wasn't quick-witted, his reflexes were good. Then he'd take out Patterson. Vague, extremely vague. This version of planning fell mostly into the category of wishful thinking.

Though Jack could hear people coming and going outside the door to the den, this room was quiet, except for Bryant's tuneless humming of a country-western song and Patterson's urgent phone conversations.

The old man was kidding himself if he thought he'd get out of this mess with his job intact. Another marshal had been brutally murdered, and that kind of error wouldn't be excused with a slap on the wrist. Jack wondered how much Rojas had paid for their treachery; he hoped it wasn't nearly enough to make up for their lost pensions.

Wearily, Patterson stood behind the desk. In the past half hour, he'd aged ten years. His jowls sagged and his eyes sunk deep in their sockets. He concluded his conversation with a crisp "Yes, sir." When he turned toward Bryant, a cold smile twisted his thin, bloodless lips. "They bought it."

Eager as a puppy, Bryant bounded toward the desk. "Are you telling me that we ain't going to get blamed for Perry being killed?"

"We'll be fine," Patterson said, "as long as you stick to the story. All you have to say is that we were asleep at the safe house, and Perry was on watch. Rojas killed him and went after Jack. Before we had time to react, it was over."

"Got it." Bryant nodded, easily satisfied. "What do we do right now?"

"We have our orders." He held his cell phone so Jack could see. "I've got a couple of emailed verifications from on high. That ought to keep your girlfriend happy."

"She's not my girlfriend," Jack said. No way did he want any repercussions to bounce back on Caitlyn. "She's just a woman who happened to be in the wrong place at the wrong time."

"But she's a reporter, and that means trouble. Not that she'll get any answers after we're gone. Everything about this case is going to turn top secret."

Jack thought he was seriously underestimating Caitlyn's abilities but said nothing. He wanted Patterson to think he was getting away clean.

Bryant asked, "What are our orders?"

"We go to a private airfield not far from here. A chopper picks us up and flies us to Colorado Springs. From there, we get a flight to Chicago."

Jack didn't like the sound of these orders. A short drive didn't give him much time to act. "How do you rate a private chopper?"

"Since Rojas is still on the loose, our situation is considered eminently dangerous." There was a flash of anger in his dulled eyes. "But you won't be riding on that chopper. Rojas is my excuse for you to be dead before we even get to the airfield."

There was a knock on the door. Danny stepped inside. Though he moved stiffly, he looked like he was well on the way to recovery. "Marshal Patterson, we have a problem."

"Now what?"

"There's an FBI agent on his way to talk to you."

"FBI," Bryant yelped.

"Our local congressman, Bob Woodley, showed up, and he's pretty peeved. He called an FBI agent he's worked with. I'm afraid if you don't humor Woodley, he'll be on the phone to the governor."

"Let him." Patterson waved his cell phone. "I have authorization to take this man into custody."

"Great," Danny said. "All you need to do is talk to Woodley. It'll only take a minute. He wants to see both of you. I'll keep an eye on your witness."

As soon as Patterson and Bryant left the room, Danny went to the window and yanked it open. "Get the hell out of here."

"Why are you doing this?" Jack asked.

"Let's just say this makes us even."

He didn't waste another second wondering why Danny had a change of heart. Jack knew the answer. Caitlyn.

Chapter Fourteen

Caitlyn was impressed with Jack's agility as he slipped through the den window into the shrubs at the side of the house. His cuffed wrists didn't hamper his movements in the least.

Without speaking, she motioned to him. As soon as he reached her side, she whispered, "Duck down and stay low. We're going to weave through these cars."

He glanced over his shoulder. "I'd rather run for open terrain. I can make it to the barn."

"No time to explain. We do it my way."

She'd already arranged with Heather to lay down a couple of false trails. Moments ago, Heather had instructed two of the ranch hands to saddle up and ride to the far pasture to check on the couple hundred head of cattle grazing in that area. Another guy was driving one of the four-wheelers toward the south end of the ranch. Caitlyn figured the marshals would be distracted by those tracks while she and Jack got away.

He followed as she crept around the eight or nine vehicles that were parked helter-skelter at the front door of the Circle L ranch house. She moved stealthily, being careful not to attract attention from the ranch hands who had gathered near the barn or the two deputies on the porch. Though she couldn't make out the words in specific conversations, she heard tension in their voices. By now, everyone was aware of the threat from Rojas.

When she got to Woodley's huge, finned, turquoise-and-cream-colored 1957 Ford Fairlane, she unlocked the trunk and pointed to the inside.

He shot her a look that was half anger and half disbelief. Then he glanced around. With all these people, he couldn't run without being seen. Grumbling, he climbed inside.

She joined him and pulled the trunk closed. The dark covered them as tightly as shrink wrap. The air smelled of gas, grease and grit. Even though this space was big for a car trunk, they were jammed together. Her legs twined with his. She couldn't find a good place to put her arms without embracing him.

"The cuffs," he said.

She dug in her jeans pocket for the key. After a bit of clumsy groping, she used the flashlight function on her cell phone so she could see well enough to unlock the cuffs.

As soon as he was free, he caught hold of her hand and turned the cell phone light so he could see her. "You combed your hair," he said, "and changed your clothes."

"Thanks for noticing."

"You look nice in blue," he whispered.

"What is this? A first date?"

Before he turned the light off, she caught a glimpse of his sexy grin. Being this close to Jack was already having a sensual effect on her. She tucked her arms over her breasts so she wouldn't be rubbing against his chest.

His upper arm draped around her with his hand resting on the small of her back. He asked, "How is Danny going to explain my escape?"

"By the time the marshals get back to the den, Danny will be upstairs in bed with his wife standing guard over him. None of the local guys are going to give him a hard time. They all think he's a hero."

Keeping her voice low, she told him about the decoy trails they'd set out for the marshals to follow. "Assuming that they're able to track in the dark. Patterson doesn't strike me as somebody who knows his way around the outdoors, but I'll bet the Texan has done his share of hunting."

"That's possible," Jack said. "There has to be something Bryant is good at."

The voices from the ranch house took on a note of urgency. There were sounds of footsteps hustling and doors being slammed. She guessed that the marshals had discovered Jack's escape. The arm he'd wrapped around her tightened protectively. She knew that they needed to be silent.

With her eyes closed, she pressed her face into the crook of his neck. His musky scent teased her nostrils. After a day on the run, he definitely didn't smell like cologne. But she didn't mind the earthy odor; it was masculine and somehow attractive. Heat radiated from his pores. His chest rose and fell as he breathed, and even that action was sexy. If she relaxed and allowed her body to melt into his, she knew she'd be overwhelmed.

Mentally, she distanced herself from him. More than once, she'd asked herself why she was so invested in Jack's rescue. The big reason was utterly apparent. He was a good man, trying to do the right thing, and he didn't deserve to be threatened, especially not by the men who were assigned to protect him. She had to fight for Jack because it was the right thing to do. Her motivations were based on truth, justice and the American way.

And it didn't hurt that he was hot. Being close to him set off a fiery chemistry that was anything but high-minded.

She didn't want to lose him, didn't want this feeling of passion to dissipate into nothingness.

Trying to get comfortable, she wriggled her legs, and he reacted with a twitch. They needed to be careful. If the Ford Fairlane started bouncing, they'd be found for sure.

The voices came closer. She thought she heard Patterson shouting angry orders. Car doors creaked open and slammed shut, but she didn't hear anyone driving away. Were they searching the cars? Someone bumped into the fender of the Fairlane, and she caught her breath to keep from making noise.

Until now, she'd been too busy planning and thinking to acknowledge the undercurrent of fear that started earlier today. If they were found, the consequences would be disastrous. She never should have gotten all these other people involved. Danny could lose his job for helping Jack escape. There might be legal charges against Heather and Woodley. As for Jack? If the marshals took him, they'd kill him. She trembled. *What have I done?*

Jack whispered in her ear, "Scared?"

Though he couldn't see her in the dark, she nodded.

"Think of something else," he said. "Something good."

That was a childish solution, like whistling in a graveyard to show the ghosts you weren't afraid. Tension squeezed her lungs. She felt a scream rising in the back of her throat.

"You have some good memories." His voice was one step up from silence. "Think of your childhood."

She remembered a summer afternoon. She was sixteen and had just gotten her driver's license. Her mom asked her to deliver a basket of muffins to Mr. Woodley's house.

Determined not to have an accident, she drove very carefully past the Circle L and went to Mr. Woodley's house. He sat on a rocker on the front porch, waiting for her. Most of her parents' friends ignored her or regarded her with the sort of suspicion and disdain adults reserved for teenagers. Mr. Woodley was different—a high school English teacher who actually enjoyed his students.

He accepted the muffins and told her to thank her mom. "Now let's get to the real reason you came to visit."

He escorted her to the computer in his spare bedroom. While they were staying at the cabin, her parents banned all use of electronics, especially the internet. Her brother and she were supposed to spend the summer appreciating nature, but she had more on her mind than gathering pinecones and wading in creeks.

A few days before, she had been at the Circle L when a mare birthed her foal. She needed to write about the experience. While she waited for the computer to boot up, she pulled a small spiral notebook from her back pocket. The pages were densely scribbled with notes, which she held up for Mr. Woodley to see. "I interviewed the veterinarian."

"That will give some depth to your story."

"And I want to talk to the ranch hands so I can get an idea of what life is going to hold for the baby horse."

"I thought you had the makings of a poet, but I see I was wrong." Mr. Woodley placed his hand on her shoulder. "Someday, you're going to be a fine journalist."

Her memory soothed the panic that had threatened to overwhelm her. Her breathing settled into a regular pattern. Caitlyn was a long way from calm, but she wasn't about to explode.

When she felt someone yanking on the door handle of the Fairlane, she was jerked back to the present. Whoever had been tugging let go with a string of curses.

Woodley's voice boomed from nearby. "Be careful, Patterson. This is a classic vehicle."

"Unlock it." Patterson's voice was terse.

"Sure thing," Woodley said. "But nobody's in there. I always keep my car locked. It's a habit."

She heard the door open. The car rocked, and she assumed that Patterson had climbed inside to look into the backseat. Silently, she prayed that he'd move on. Their hiding place in the trunk seemed as obvious as a wrapped birthday present with a big red bow.

Patterson growled, "You've caused me a lot of trouble, old man."

"Let's talk it over with my friend from the FBI. He ought to be here any minute."

"I don't have time to waste with the FBI." He raised his voice. "Bryant, I'm over here."

In a breathless rush, the Texan said, "I was in the barn. Think we got a trail to follow. There's a couple of horses gone from their stalls."

"I should have known," Patterson muttered. "He took off on horseback. Again."

A moment passed. The sounds of the searchers became more distant. The door of the Ford Fairlane opened. The car jostled as someone got behind the steering wheel. The engine started. As the car went in reverse, she heard Mr. Woodley say, "On our way. Over the river and through the woods."

They'd pulled it off. A clean getaway.

HIDING IN THE TRUNK of a car wasn't the most manly way to escape, but Jack didn't mind. The ancient suspension system in the old Ford bounced Caitlyn against him with every bump they hit, and there were a lot of bumps on the graded gravel roads. They probably hadn't traveled a mile before her clenched arms loosened up, and she accidentally smacked him with the handcuffs she still held.

"Give me those," he said.

"Can't see where you are. I'll stick them in the pocket of this lovely blue jacket that's probably going to be filthy by the time I get out of the trunk."

"That'd be a shame." He hadn't been lying when he told her she looked pretty.

After one huge jolt, she started to giggle. Her unbridled laughter was as bright as the inside of the trunk was dark. Her legs tangled with his, accidentally rubbing against his thighs and groin. They were bumping apart and grinding together. It was like making love in a blender.

On a relatively smooth stretch of road, he asked, "Do you mind telling me where we're going?"

"I considered riding all the way to Denver," she said. "But there's too much going on in this area. The manhunt for Rojas is massive. The police have heavy-duty surveillance and roadblocks. The car could be stopped and searched."

And he didn't dare turn himself over to anyone in law enforcement. No matter what they thought, they'd be obliged to take him into custody and turn him over to Patterson. "I don't expect the cops are going to be happy about my escape from the Circle L."

She bumped against his chest. "Probably not."

"You never answered my question."

"Do you really want to know where we're going?" she teased. "Wouldn't you rather sit back and let me take care of every little thing?"

He had to admit that she'd done a good job of springing him from Patterson's custody. She was a problem solver, smart and competent. But he liked being the one in charge. "Tell me."

"Or else? How are you going to make me talk?"

He knew what he'd like to do. With her body rubbing up

against him in many inappropriate places, there was one predominant thought in his mind. He held her tight.

"Here's what I'll do to you, babe. First, I'm going to kiss you until your lips are numb. Then I'm going to take off that blue jacket and unbutton your shirt. And I'm going to grab you here." He lowered his hand and squeezed her butt. "You're going to be putty. You'll tell me everything I want to know."

"Bob Woodley's house," she peeped. "That's where we're headed."

"Woodley? The guy who owns this car?" If the Ford Fairlane was any indication, he didn't think Woodley's house would be safe. People who lived in the past tended to be less than vigilant when it came to the present.

"He told me that he was robbed last year, and he put in a state-of-the-art security system."

Jack doubted that good old Bob Woodley could guarantee their safety, but he needed a place to rest, recuperate and eat something more substantial than energy bars. Since last night, he'd caught only a few hours' sleep in the cavern. His body still ached with old bruises. Whenever he recalled the wound on the back of his head, it answered him with a quiet throb.

The car stopped and the engine went quiet. He heard the sound of a mechanical garage door closing.

The trunk opened. After being in darkness, the overhead bulb in the two-car garage glared like a klieg light. Untangling himself from Caitlyn took a moment and unleashed another burst of giggles from her.

Finally, Jack was on his feet. The first thing he noticed was that the second car in the garage was a Land Rover that couldn't have been more than two or three years old—a sensible vehicle for someone who lived in the mountains. A tool bench at the back of the garage displayed a neat array of power tools. Apparently, the old man had an organized side to his personality. Caitlyn had spoken fondly of Woodley. A retired English teacher. A friend of her parents.

He faced the rangy, white-haired stranger who had played a pivotal role in his rescue. Though there weren't sufficient words to thank him, Jack said, "I appreciate what you've done."

Woodley assessed him with a stern gaze. "You're the fellow who caused all this trouble."

Jack held out his hand. "Call me Jack."

"That's not your real name." With a firm grip, Woodley shook his hand. "I don't cotton to men who hide behind aliases. Let's use your real name. Nick Racine."

Chapter Fifteen

Jack wasn't often caught off guard. His natural wariness kept him on his toes, ready to react to any threat. The name Nick Racine was dangerous. As soon as Woodley spoke it, Jack thought of plausible excuses for the alias. Deception was second nature to him, but he couldn't look this good man in the eye and lie to him. More important, Jack wanted—no, needed—to be truthful with Caitlyn.

She eyed him suspiciously then focused on Woodley. "Where did you hear that name?"

"From my friend in the FBI. He's one of my former students, and he doesn't have any reason to lie to me."

"What did he say?"

"He spoke to the marshal on the phone." Woodley scowled. "By the way, that Patterson fellow is rude and unpleasant. I try to see the best in people, but that guy was shifty."

"Agreed," Caitlyn said briskly. "And then?"

"My young FBI friend warned me that there wasn't much he could do to stop the marshals. That was when he mentioned the name Nick Racine." He stared hard at Jack. "I thought it strange because Caitlyn called you something else."

When she turned her gaze on Jack, she'd switched into her journalist persona. Her eyes were clear. Her attitude, cool. She was nothing like the soft woman who had been giggling in the trunk of the Ford Fairlane and rubbing up against him. "Have you ever heard the name Nick Racine before?"

He didn't connect with that identity and he sure as hell didn't believe the stories Bryant had been spouting about his supposedly legendary deeds. If he truly was a one-man strike force, shouldn't he be able to remember? "Bryant and Patterson said I was Nick Racine."

"I thought you were Tony Perez."

So did I. He shrugged. There wasn't anything he could say to clarify his identity.

"We need to look into this." She pivoted and marched toward the side door in the garage. "I'll need to use the computer."

"Hold on," Woodley said. "Who's Tony Perez? Why in blazes doesn't this man know his own name?"

She came back and stood before him. "The important thing for you to know is that this man—I'm going to call him Jack—is a decent human being. He risked his life to rescue Danny, and he saved me from a gang of men with guns." She took both of Woodley's hands in hers. "I trust Jack. And I'm asking you to do the same."

The way he looked at Caitlyn reminded Jack of an affectionate uncle with his fair-haired niece. The old man was proud of her accomplishments. "You've grown up to be quite a woman. I always knew you'd turn out okay."

"You were one of the first people who believed in me. You encouraged me to be a journalist."

"It's not hard to pick out a diamond in a bowl of sand." He gave her a wink and turned to Jack. "All right, young man. If Caitlyn vouches for you, I've got to accept you. With all your fake names."

"Thank you, sir."

"Now," she said, "lead me to the computer."

Woodley circled around the car and went to the door. "Are you two hungry?"

"Starved," Caitlyn said. "You know what I really want? When you used to come over to our cabin and play Scrabble with Mom and Dad, you always made grilled cheese sandwiches and tomato soup for me and my brother. Comfort food."

"Coming right up," he said, "but I don't want you two in the kitchen with me. There are too many lights, too many windows and too many people looking for you."

Jack appreciated Woodley's caution. Rojas was still at large. And Patterson might decide to come here after he was done with his wild goose chase. Jack followed Caitlyn and Woodley through the door that led directly into the house.

Woodley said, "I don't want to turn on any lights."

Again, Jack approved. Moonlight through the windows provided enough illumination to find their way through a living room and down a hallway. In a small bedroom, Woodley turned on the overhead light.

The windows were covered with shades and curtains. The decor was a mixture of antique and high-tech. A laptop computer rested on a carved oak, rolltop desk with a matching office chair. Wooden bookshelves held the eclectic collection of an avid reader, ranging from poetry to electronics manuals. A patchwork quilt covered the double bed with a curlicue brass frame. One corner was devoted to surveillance and security.

"Here's where you'll be sleeping, Jack." The old man went to the security equipment and flipped a couple of switches. "These four infrared screens show the outdoor views of my property. The garage, front door, northern side and western. The back of the house butts up to a hillside and is inaccessible. I've activated the motion sensors at a twenty-yard perimeter around the house and the burglar alarm in case anybody jiggles the door or busts a window."

In the unformed memories of his past, Jack knew he'd seen similar security arrangements. "This is a sophisticated system. Did you install it yourself?"

"It's overkill," Woodley admitted. "When I got robbed, I was so ticked off that I set this place up as a fortress, mostly because I enjoyed fiddling around with the electronics."

"He's always been that way," Caitlyn said. She'd already positioned herself at the desk where she opened the laptop. "If he hadn't been an English teacher, Mr. Woodley would have been a mechanic."

"And a damn good one—good enough to keep my 1957 Ford Fairlane in running condition."

Jack liked the old guy—a man who could work with his hands and with his mind. "I'm impressed."

"And you're going to be even more excited by my grilled cheese sandwiches. Before I head out to the kitchen, there's one more thing I need to show you." He stepped into the hallway and pointed at a closed door. "This is going to be Caitlyn's bedroom. Understand?"

"Yes, sir." Jack had been hoping they'd have to sleep in the same room, preferably in the same bed. No such luck.

He closed the door behind Woodley and went to the rolltop desk, where Caitlyn sat hunched over the computer. Her fingers skipped across the keyboard as she started her identity search. "Should I look for Nicholas Racine or Nick?"

"Neither. I'm not Nick Racine."

"Other people seem to think you are. We need to research the possibilities."

Buried deep in the back of his mind was something akin to dread; he didn't want to be Nick Racine. Uncovering that identity would cause no end of pain. "I have a better idea. Look up Tony Perez."

In a couple of minutes, she'd accessed a site that showed his mug shot. His hair was longer, as were his sideburns, and he had a soul patch on his chin.

"That's you," Caitlyn said. "Love the facial hair."

He massaged the spot between his lower lip and his chin that was now rough with stubble. "That settles it. We know my real identity."

"Do you remember being Tony Perez?"

He had a crystal clear memory of watching Mark Santoro die and of being shot. "I remember some things."

She pointed to the computer screen. "This is your address in Chicago. Tell me about the place where you lived."

Her voice was firm and demanding. Bossy, in fact. And he wasn't inclined to take orders. "Are you interviewing me?"

"I'm looking for answers, yes."

"What's the point? We know Rojas wants to kill me to keep me from testifying. He paid off the marshals, and they need me dead so they can keep their jobs. Those are the facts. My name isn't going to change them."

She rose from the desk chair and faced him. Curiosity shone in her eyes. The color of her jacket emphasized the deep blue of her irises. "Don't you want to know who you are?"

"I like being Jack Dalton." A man without a past had no regrets.

"Please cooperate."

"Are you asking because you care or because you're a reporter?"

"I'll admit that you're a damn good story. And I suppose I could say that I care about you." With her thumb and index finger she measured an inch. "Maybe this much."

"Not much incentive."

She rolled her eyes. "Has anyone ever told you that you're a giant pain in the butt?"

"I'd like to answer that question but, damn…" He shot her a grin. "I just don't remember."

"Tell me about the place where you lived in Chicago," she repeated.

He tore his gaze away from her and paced as though moving around would jog his memory. "It was a one-bedroom apartment in an older building with an ancient elevator. I was on the third floor." A picture took shape in his mind. "Brown sofa. Television. Wood table full of clutter. I had a king-size bed. I like big beds."

"Did you have a girlfriend to share that bed?"

In his mind, he saw a woman with long hair and too much eye makeup. "A blonde. That's my type. Blondes with long legs. Kind of like you."

"Lucky me," she said. "Keep talking."

"The woman in Chicago wasn't anything special. We dated." And she had spent a few hours in his king-size bed. "She was no big deal."

"Where did you live before that?"

In the corner of the room, he stared at the surveillance screens that surrounded the house. In infrared view, the trunks of pine trees were ghostly shadows. "There isn't time for us to work backward through my rental history. What do you really want to know?"

"I've never interviewed someone with amnesia. I'm trying to find the key that makes you remember."

"Tony Perez. I grew up in southern California." His biography flashed before him as clearly and neatly as though it had been written out on a sheet of paper. He filled in details about growing up in foster care and never knowing his parents. He'd gotten in trouble as a kid for stealing cars and shoplifting. "I lived in Arizona for a while. How am I doing?"

"Considering that you started from zero, I'm surprised. You remember a lot."

He had details. He could visualize his driver's license and recite his Social Security number. But none of it seemed real. His identity as Tony Perez seemed like something he'd seen in a movie, but he wasn't making it up. "Remembering isn't the kind of relief I thought it would be."

"How did you make a living?"

He recited a string of menial jobs. "Then I hooked up with Santoro. I collected his debts."

"An enforcer," she said. "That makes sense. I've seen you in action, and you can be very intimidating."

"I'm not a thug." He didn't want her to think of him that way. "Getting people to do what you want is more about attitude than actual violence. I developed a reputation. People were scared of me. That threat was enough."

"There had to be a reason why they were afraid. What was your reputation based on?"

"Word of mouth and a couple of well-placed lies."

He went to the bed, propped the dark blue pillows against the headboard and took off his boots so he wouldn't get the patchwork quilt dirty. Then he leaned back against the pillows with his legs stretched out straight in front of him. For the first time today, he allowed himself to relax. God, he was tired.

Caitlyn perched on the edge of the bed beside his legs, positioning herself so she wasn't touching him. "I'm interested in how you set yourself up as a dangerous person."

"First you've got to build a reputation. Other people

have to say you're tough. In Chicago, I used a snitch and a couple of cops. The stories they told made me sound like a cold-blooded sadist."

"Cops? How did you get them to lie for you?"

"Give them something they want. A bribe. A promise. A gift. Just like Rojas got Patterson to work for him."

"Then what?" she asked.

"You need to prove yourself. I picked the biggest, toughest guy in the gang and took him down. I didn't kill him or do any permanent damage, but I hurt him enough that he knew I could have killed him. In a way, he owed me his life."

"Keep your enemies close." She regarded him thoughtfully. "This is beginning to sound like Sun Tzu, *The Art of War.*"

"All warfare is deception," he quoted.

"Your life as Tony Perez sounds complicated. Why would you go through such an elaborate setup?"

A good question. "I was in a new town. I needed to get close to power. That's what I do." He laced his fingers behind his head and leaned back. Exhaustion tugged at his eyelids.

"Okay, you established your reputation and you proved yourself," she said. "What next?"

"I needed an ally. Somebody who had my back. That was Mark Santoro. When I first met him, I was using him. But he became a friend."

Santoro wasn't a saint. Pretty much the opposite. He was a head man in a drug-running crime family, but he was loyal to his crew and strong-willed. He had a family—twin girls who would grow up without their father.

"You still grieve for him," she said.

"His death was unnecessary and pointless," he said. "I

should have seen the attack coming, should have known what Rojas was planning."

"How could you know?"

"It was my job."

"Protecting your boss?" she asked.

Though he nodded, he knew there was something more. Only a few hours ago, Greg Rojas looked him in the eye and called him Nick Racine. Jack had been so startled that he lost his chance to shoot in spite of his need for revenge. He wanted Rojas to suffer for the part he'd played in the death of Mark Santoro and for… There was another name, another person.

An intense rage exploded behind his eyelids in a blinding fireball. Someone else had been murdered. He had to remember. Until he knew that name, his soul was empty. His life had no meaning.

There was a reason he had played this complicated charade with Mark Santoro.

"Jack?" He heard Caitlyn calling him back to reality. "Jack, are you all right?"

He had to find the answers, and he knew where to start. "We need more information on Nick Racine."

Chapter Sixteen

Near midnight, Jack lay on his back and stared up at the ceiling above the bed. His body floated in a sea of exhaustion, but his mind wouldn't succumb to sleep. The surveillance screens in the corner cast an eerie, gray light across the flat surface. His memories took shape.

He saw the number eight on the scuffed beige door of the motel room. The night was heavy, dark and cold. The red-haired man unlocked door number eight and walked inside carrying a black gym bag.

Jack blinked. He knew what came next, knew he should close his eyes, but he couldn't stop himself from staring as the scene played out. He watched himself.

He parked a block away and crept toward a clump of leafless shrubs at the edge of the motel parking lot. There, he waited impatiently with his Beretta M9 automatic. This wasn't murder; it was an execution for a man who lived outside the law. His name was Eric Deaver. He'd done unspeakable things.

The curtains in room number eight didn't close all the way. Through the gap, he saw the flicker from a television screen. Was Eric Deaver lying on the bed? Laughing at lame jokes from late-night talk-show hosts?

The door flung open. Red-haired Deaver was silhou-

etted in the frame. He gripped guns with both hands. He
bellowed, "I know you're here."

One shot. One bullet. In the center of his forehead. It
was over. Justice was served.

Still caught up in his memory, Jack heard the knob on
his bedroom door click. He bolted from the bed, ready to
fight to the death.

CAITLYN PAUSED WITH her hand on the doorknob. Entering Jack's bedroom might be a really foolish move. She
shifted her weight, and the floorboards creaked. Maybe she
should trot back to her bedroom and put on more clothes.
Not that the oversize T-shirt and terry-cloth bathrobe she'd
borrowed from Woodley counted as a seductive negligee,
but she didn't want Jack to get the wrong idea.

I'm not going to have sex with him. She'd known Jack
for only a day. From the little he'd told her about his past,
he was a scary guy. And there was absolutely no chance of
any future relationship. She didn't want him to think that
appearing at his bedroom door was some kind of booty
call. There would be no lovemaking. She did, however,
intend to sleep in the same room as him.

If she left him alone, she was certain that he wouldn't
be here in the morning. He'd made it clear that he didn't
want to work with a partner because of the unknown, the
intensity, the danger, blah, blah, blah. She wasn't going to
be shuffled aside. If he was going to run, she'd be at his
side. He was her story, and she intended to follow him to
the conclusion.

Twisting the knob, she opened the door and poked her
head inside. Before she had a chance to whisper his name,
he'd grabbed her around the throat. His arm was steel.
She couldn't move, couldn't breathe, felt herself losing
consciousness.

When he suddenly released his grip, she fell to the floor, gasping.

"Never," he said, "never sneak up on me like that."

She coughed. "What was I supposed to do?"

"Knock."

Though he was right and she really didn't expect an apology, he could have at least helped her to her feet. Instead, he went to the security corner and stared at the screens. Unspeaking, he kept his back toward her. Hostility rolled off from his wide, muscular shoulders in waves.

She stood, turned on the overhead light and padded to his bed where she sat on the edge. She adjusted her bathrobe to cover her breasts. As extra protection, she was still wearing her sports bra. "I'm sorry I couldn't find anything about Nick Racine on the internet."

"Not your fault," he muttered.

She'd tried. As a journalist, she'd learned how to use the computer to track down leads, and she'd employed every bit of her skill to locate information on Nick Racine. She'd hopscotched through databases, scanned websites and probed blogs. Though she'd found plenty of people named Nick Racine, none fit his description. "The identity should have showed up somewhere. In a credit file or bank record or work history. It's almost like Nick Racine was erased."

"It's possible," he said without turning around.

Glaring at his backside, she got distracted by the snug fit of his black jersey boxer shorts. His legs were long, muscular and masculine, with just the right amount of black hair. His bare feet and long toes looked oddly vulnerable.

She tucked her own feet—in sensible white cotton socks—up under her. "We need to make plans for tomorrow. I'm sure Mr. Woodley won't kick us out, but the marshals are going to be canvassing the area."

"I'll be gone before first light."

She noticed that he hadn't included her in his plans. "I'm coming with you."

He pivoted and came toward her. The fact that he wasn't wearing a lot of clothing made him seem bigger and more intimidating. Stubble outlined his jaw. His black eyebrows pulled down in an angry scowl. "There's no reason for you to be in danger."

"I was embedded with the troops. I can handle it."

"This is different," he said. "Use Woodley's contact at the FBI. Put yourself in his protection until Rojas is under lock and key."

An hour ago, Woodley had gotten an update on the police activity. The safe house had been secured and four men arrested after a shoot-out. Rojas and two of his men had escaped. "What if he isn't caught?"

"That means he's out of the country, and you'll never see him again."

"What are you going to do?"

His chin lifted. "It's better if you don't know."

She wasn't ready to let go. There were too many unanswered questions. "I'll decide what's best for me."

There was something different about him, but she couldn't exactly put her finger on it. A heaviness? A dark, brooding anger? He said, "This isn't your fight."

"Earlier, you asked if I was interested in you because you're a good story. Well, you're right. You're on the run, a witness in a gangland murder and a victim of unscrupulous federal officers. And let's not forget the amnesia angle. Jack, if I can get inside your head and write your story, I could be looking at a Pulitzer."

"You want inside my head?"

"That's right," she said.

"You're not going to like what you find." He lowered

himself into the desk chair and leaned forward, his elbows resting on his knees. The focus in his green eyes was painfully sharp. "I killed a man."

A murder confession? That wasn't what she wanted to hear. She held herself tightly under control, refusing to flinch. "Are you sure? What did you remember?"

"I saw the bullet pierce his skull, saw the light go out in his eyes. And I was glad to execute the bastard. I felt no guilt, no regret."

This memory wasn't consistent with what she'd seen of Jack. In dealing with the men at the safe house, he hadn't opened fire and gunned them down. His behavior was logical and precise; he didn't act like a killer. "Who was he?"

"I know his name," he said, "but I don't know why I needed to end his life. I believe the reason is tied to Rojas."

"Why?"

Though he was looking right at her, his gaze was distant. "I keep replaying that moment when I had the drop on Rojas and didn't shoot. It wasn't an ethical concern that kept me from pulling the trigger. I could have winged him without killing him."

From what she'd seen, he was a good marksman and his reflexes were lightning fast. No doubt he could have disabled Rojas and Kelso with surgical precision. "Why didn't you shoot?"

"He yelled out the name Nick Racine, as though he recognized me. And something clicked inside my head. Everything was clear. The confusion and sorrow and rage I'd been carrying around for years vanished in a puff of smoke. I knew. Knew the answer."

His voice had fallen to a hush. If she hadn't already been intrigued by him, this moment would have captured her interest. What had become clear to him? What truth had he learned? She dared not speak and break the profound silence.

"Gregorio Rojas is the answer," he said, "but I don't know the question. I need to figure it out."

"You seem to be remembering more pieces of your past all the time. If you're patient, it'll come to you."

He shook his head. "I was on this quest long before I lost my memory. It's the reason I went to work for Santoro, the reason I agreed to testify. Somehow, all of what's happened ties together."

She had to get to the bottom of this. Never in her career had she been issued such a clear challenge. "Where should we start?"

He rose from the chair, took her hand and pulled her to her feet. With gallantry unbefitting a man dressed only in jockey shorts and a T-shirt, he escorted her to the door. "Go back to bed. We both need our sleep."

"Promise you won't leave without me."

"I won't lie to you." For a moment, the hint of a smile touched his mouth and she thought he was going to kiss her, but he turned and went to his bed. As he stretched out on the sheets, he said, "Good night, Caitlyn."

Trying to get rid of me? It's not that easy, Jack. She went to the bed and leaned over him, close enough to kiss but not touching. "I'm glad you won't lie to me."

"I owe you that much."

"Actually, quite a bit more." She reached into the pocket of her bathrobe and took out the handcuffs. In one swift click, she fastened one around his right wrist and the other around her left. "You won't be going anywhere without me."

His gaze went to the steel cuffs, then to her face. His

sexy grin spread slowly. "If you wanted to sleep with me, all you had to do was ask."

"We're only going to sleep." It took an effort to hold on to that resolution while she was this close to him, but she was determined.

"I don't believe you." His voice was warm, intimate, seductive. "If you wanted to keep me here, you could have handcuffed me to this fancy brass bed frame."

"As if you couldn't pick the lock? No way. Hooking us together is the only way I can be sure where you are."

She showed him the key to the cuffs. Then she stuck her hand inside her bathrobe and T-shirt, tucking the key safely into her sports bra.

"Do you really think that's going to stop me?"

"I know you won't hurt me."

"You're right, babe." He caught hold of her right arm and pulled her down on top on him. "This won't hurt a bit."

The bathrobe tangled around her legs as she struggled to get away from him, and she was reminded of how their bodies bounced against each other during that crazy ride in the trunk of the Ford Fairlane. There was no way to avoid touching him. She knew this would happen. How could she not know? What had she been thinking?

The answer was obvious. Maybe, just maybe, she didn't want to escape. Maybe she'd come to him hoping that he'd make love to her. The magnetism between them was undeniable. Why shouldn't she relent?

"No," she said, speaking as much to herself as to him. "This is what you want."

He undid the tie on the bathrobe and pushed it out of the way. He was on top of her. Through the thin fabric of her T-shirt, she felt his body heat, and the warmth tempted her. She felt herself melting.

His face was inches away from hers. If she kissed him,

she knew this battle would be over. She wouldn't be able to stop herself.

She twisted her head on the pillow so she was looking away from him, staring at the wall beside the bed. Through clenched teeth, she said, "Stop it. I mean now."

He rolled off her. They were lying beside each other with their cuffed wrists in the middle.

"Can't blame me for getting the wrong idea," he said. "When a woman comes into your bedroom in the middle of the night with a set of handcuffs—"

"I know what this looks like." Excitement made her voice shaky; she couldn't stop her heart from throbbing. "I'm using the handcuffs for professional reasons."

"And what profession might that be?"

"I'm a reporter, and you're a story. If I want to get my career in order, I need to show that I can be an effective investigative journalist. You understand what I'm saying, I know you do. You're the one who told me I was going to be okay, that all I needed was to believe in myself."

"That wasn't much of a deduction," he said. "Anybody who's met you knows you're smart enough to accomplish great things."

"But I was scared. Paralyzed. I didn't believe in myself."

She'd hidden at her cabin like a hermit. When her position in the Middle East was cut, she knew it wasn't because she was doing a bad job. The decision was based on budgets and revenue. Still, she couldn't help feeling that she'd failed. Not anymore.

Jack's story had all the hooks that readers love, from involvement with a crime family to being on the run to corruption within the marshals. Not to mention his mysterious past. His story was worth a whole book or a miniseries, and she'd be the one to write it. She'd be damned if she would miss a single minute.

"You're right, Caitlyn. I believe in you."

His surprising moments of sensitivity made it even harder to resist him. "If we're going to get a good night's sleep, we should turn off the lights."

She climbed out of the bed, pulling him behind her with the handcuffs. She hit the light switch, and the bedroom faded into the half darkness. The glow from the surveillance screens lit their way back to the bed.

Finding a comfortable position with their hands cuffed together wasn't easy. They both ended up on their sides, facing each other. In the dim light, she saw that his eyes were closed. His lashes were long, thick and black. Any woman would kill for eyelashes like that. But there was nothing feminine about his face. Not with the stubble that outlined his sexy mouth. Not with his strong cheekbones and jaw.

Sleep was the furthest thing from her mind. She asked, "Do we have a plan for tomorrow?"

"No particular plan, just a couple of ideas. I figured I'd stick around this area. Do some investigating."

"Shouldn't you be focused on escape?"

"There's still three days before the trial. I want to use that time."

"How did you plan on getting around?"

"Woodley has a nice little ATV in a shed behind the garage and I—"

"You can't steal his four-wheeler," she said firmly. "After the risk he took for you, how could you even think of hijacking his property?"

His eyelids opened. "Woodley and I already talked about it. He gave me the keys."

"Well, good." She shouldn't have accused him. No

matter what had happened in his past, Jack was far too loyal to betray the people who treated him right. "I can ride on the back of the ATV. You'll be glad you brought me along. I can guide you through the backcountry."

For a long moment, he gazed at her. A deep sense of yearning urged her toward him. She wanted to touch him, to glide into his embrace. Physically, he was everything she wanted in a man—tall, lean and muscular. She even liked the scars she knew were under his T-shirt.

"Tell me the reason," he said, "that we can't make love."

"I don't know who you are—Tony or Nick or someone else altogether."

"You know me as Jack."

She certainly did. He was the stranger who showed up on her doorstep, the man who saved her life and believed in her. "It's only been a day."

"A matter of timing."

Though she didn't have silly rules, such as not kissing on the first date, she didn't want to rush into lovemaking. Intimacy was a risk she wasn't ready to take. "Timing is important."

"Tomorrow," he said, "we'll have known each other twice as long. That should be enough."

She closed her eyes and pretended to sleep.

Chapter Seventeen

Though the curtains and shades over the bedroom windows blocked out the light, Jack sensed that it was close to dawn. His inner alarm clock, which he considered more accurate than a Swiss timepiece, told him that he'd been in bed for five hours. He lifted his head from the pillow and craned his neck to see the digital clock on the desk. Four forty-seven. Time to get moving.

In spite of the handcuffs, he'd slept well. The cozy presence of a woman in his bed reminded him of what normal life was all about. Her scent, the little kitten sounds she made in her sleep and the way her body occasionally rubbed against him made him feel alive. He looked over at Caitlyn. His eyes had become accustomed to the dim light from the surveillance screens, and he could see fairly well. Her bathrobe was open and her long T-shirt had hiked up, giving him an unfettered view of her long, firm legs. One knee was bent, and her toes pointed like a ballerina midleap. Her free arm arched above her head. For a slender woman, she took up a lot of space. He grinned. *Bed hog.*

Leaning over her, he studied the delicate angles of her face from the sweep of her eyebrows to the tip of her chin. Her straight blond hair fell in wisps across her cheeks. Her lips parted slightly, and her breathing was slow and steady. She was still asleep.

Her need to follow him and get his whole story was understandable, and he appreciated her dedication to her career. But he'd rather work alone. If he could unfasten the handcuff and slip away before she missed him, that would be all for the best. The trick would be to retrieve the key from her bra without waking her up.

He lightly touched the bare skin below her collarbone. Her breathing didn't change. Beneath her shapeless T-shirt, her chest rose and fell in a steady pattern.

Slowly, slowly, he moved his fingertips toward the valley between her breasts. He'd been in custody since he was shot, hadn't been anywhere near a woman for five months. Her skin was soft and warm, enticing him. He wanted to touch her all over, to taste her mouth, her throat, the tips of her breasts. He wanted her legs wrapped around him. Her arms, clinging to him. Her idea of waiting for a specific number of hours or days or weeks before making love was ridiculous. They were consenting adults, obviously attracted to each other. Why the hell shouldn't they seize the moment?

Under her T-shirt, he felt the edge of her sports bra. Just a little lower…

Her eyelids snapped open. "Are you trying to cop a feel or grab the key?"

"Both."

"How about neither?" She pushed his hand away. "Go back to sleep."

"It's time to go. Unless you want to watch me pee, you should unlock the cuffs."

"Ew. I'm not following you into the bathroom." As she fished the key from her bra, she glanced at the clock. "It's not even five o'clock."

"You could stay here and sleep in."

"Not an option," she said. "But this is really, really early. Do we have to leave now?"

"I promised Woodley I'd be gone before he got out of bed. If the police come knocking, he can honestly say that he has no idea where I went."

"Fine." She unlocked the cuffs and rubbed the red circle on her wrist. "I get the bathroom first."

"Hurry."

"Less than five minutes," she promised.

"Don't turn on any lights," he warned. Though Woodley's security system hadn't sounded an alert, it didn't hurt to be careful. *Always plan for the worst-case scenario.* The marshals could be staking out the house.

Jack doubted that Rojas was still in the area. A wealthy man like him was able to pay for an arranged escape. He probably had a private chopper on call.

After her allotted five minutes, Caitlyn peeked in to tell him she was done, and he took his turn. Though he would have liked to shave, he followed his own warning and kept the lights in the bathroom off. Back in his bedroom, he dressed in a fresh T-shirt and jeans provided by Woodley. The old man had also given Jack a lightweight canvas jacket in khaki. The keys to the ATV were in the front pocket.

Caitlyn joined him. She'd yanked her hair into a ponytail and thrown on the clothes she'd worn last night. The blue jacket was grungy from being in the car trunk, but she still looked fresh and awake.

Together, they went down the hallway, pretending that they hadn't made enough noise to wake their host. Jack hoped Woodley's taste in all-terrain vehicles didn't mirror his love of vintage cars.

Circling the house, they entered the shed behind the garage, closed the door and turned on the light. The two-person ATV wasn't brand-new but probably less than ten years old. The dents and scratches on the frame indicated that Woodley had ridden this four-wheeler hard, but Jack trusted the man who liked mechanics to keep all his vehicles in good running order. A blue helmet rested on the well-worn front seat. The lid on the storage container behind the second seat was propped open, and Caitlyn looked inside.

"This is so sweet," she said. "He packed a sleeping bag, a canteen and some food for you."

"Woodley's a good man."

She started searching thought the other outdoor gear in the shed. "He didn't know I'd be coming along. We need to find another sleeping bag and helmet. Maybe a tent in case we need to set up camp."

"We're not going on a field trip."

"Which brings up an important question," she said. "Where exactly are we going?"

The best way for him to figure out why he'd executed the red-haired man was to learn more about Nick Racine. The name still didn't resonate with him. He had hoped the hours of sleep might heal the holes in his memory, but no such luck. He needed to investigate.

Since Patterson and Bryant had identified him as Racine when he was in their custody, Jack thought he might find clues at the place where they'd held him. "We're going back to the safe house."

She found a second blue helmet which she plopped on her head. "But it's a crime scene. Mr. Woodley said the police had their shoot-out with the Rojas men there. Won't the area be closed off?"

"We'll see."

She stuffed a second sleeping bag into the carrier and closed the lid. "Have you ever driven an ATV before?"

"Oh, yeah."

During the time he spent in the desert with his mentor, they used dune buggies to get around. This ATV—with its solid frame and seriously heavy-duty tires—was the muscular big brother of those dune buggies. Jack was looking forward to riding over the hillsides. Pushing hard, he wheeled the ATV out of the shed and locked the door behind him.

"Don't forget your helmet," she said.

"Colorado doesn't have a helmet law."

"Humor me." She shoved the helmet into his hands. "We're in enough danger without getting into a crash and busting our heads open."

Helmet in place, he climbed onto the seat. Caitlyn mounted behind him. Her arms weren't wrapped around him like they'd be on a dirt bike, but she was close enough to lean forward and tap the back of his helmet.

He turned his head. "What was that for?"

"Just excited," she said. "Let her rip."

He turned the key in the ignition. The engine roared as he drove away, threading his way through the tree trunks, heading uphill and away from the road. In the thin light before the dawn, he couldn't see clearly and had to move at a slow pace through the forest. It was difficult to gauge distances, and he added a couple more dents to the frame of the ATV.

At the crest of the ridge above Woodley's house, she flicked her fingers against his helmet and said, "You should go east. That's to your right. And head downhill."

He might have guessed as much, but he was glad to have her confirmation. The ATV rumbled along a narrow path, louder than a Harley. This vehicle wasn't made for stealth; they'd have to park a distance away from the safe house and approach on foot.

As they meandered through the trees, the rising sun

painted the sky in tones of pale pink and yellow, streaked with the long wisps of cirrus clouds. The dawn light gave form to the rising hills and dark forests.

When they came to a meadow, the wide-open space beckoned to him. After picking his way cautiously, he wanted to go fast. He gunned the engine and floored it. They were flying, careening over the uneven terrain with the fresh wind whipping around them. He felt free. Behind him, Caitlyn yelped and laughed in sheer exhilaration.

At the far side of the meadow, she tapped his helmet again. "Jack, you need to stop."

He pulled onto a flat space and killed the engine.

Immediately, she jumped off the back seat and took off her helmet. She winced and rubbed at her tailbone. "Ow, ow, ow."

"Are you okay?"

"Going over those ruts, I really whacked my bottom." She stretched and groaned and stretched again. "I'm fine. It's nothing a good massage won't fix."

"I'd volunteer for that job."

"I bet you would."

The light of a new day glimmered in her blond hair, and she beamed a smile. The combination of nature's awesome beauty and Caitlyn's lively energy delighted him. His blood was still rushing with the sensation of speed. He was... happy.

He dropped his gaze, knowing that he'd felt this way before. As Nick or Tony or Jack or whoever the hell he was, he had experienced happiness. A dangerous emotion often followed by despair. "How far are we from the safe house?"

She approached him. "What's wrong?"

"I want to get there before it's too late."

"We're not far," she said. "I can't give you exact coordinates, but the safe house and Mr. Woodley's place are both to the east of Pinedale. From the top of that ridge, we ought to be able to get our bearings."

After she got back onto the ATV, he headed toward the high point. His skill in maneuvering had improved to the extent that he only ran over one small shrub on the way.

She tapped his helmet. "Park here."

He turned off the engine, dismounted and took off the helmet. "You've got to stop flicking my helmet."

She shrugged. "I used to do that with one of my drivers in the Middle East. We were covered in protective gear, and tapping his helmet was the best way to get his attention."

"I don't like it." He hiked uphill to the edge of the cliff. A long view spread before him. To the south, he saw the main road and the turnoff to the safe house. Surrounding trees blocked his view of the house itself.

Standing beside him, Caitlyn bragged, "Am I good or what?"

Without her knowledge of the area, he could have been wandering these mountains for hours. "You have an impressive sense of direction."

"I used to ride over here to visit Mr. Woodley and then go exploring. Never once did I get lost."

That dangerous happiness lingered inside him, and he realized that she was a big part of that feeling. Though she could be irritating and aggressive, she challenged him in a good way. He wanted to pull her into his arms for a hug. Instead, he teased, "You have the instincts of a bloodhound."

"Are you calling me a dog?"

"I'm saying that it's no wonder you turned out to be a reporter. You always find your way."

She leaned her back against a boulder and folded her arms below her breasts. "Getting close to the safe house is going to be a problem. We can't muffle the engine noise. And it's getting lighter by the minute."

Though it couldn't have been much past five-thirty, the sun was rising fast. "If anybody's at the safe house, we'll turn back. If not, the noise won't matter."

"I can't believe the police left the place abandoned," she said. "Don't they need to process the crime scene?"

"Real life isn't like the movies. In most cases, there isn't a crack team of CSI investigators on hand. I'd expect the local law enforcement to be occupied with their manhunt. The search for Rojas."

"And for you." She pushed herself away from the boulder and came closer to him. "I've been thinking. Would it be so bad to turn yourself in?"

"I'm not going anywhere with the marshals."

"You don't have to," she said. "After the sheriff has taken a look at the safe house, Patterson and Bryant won't have much credibility. No matter what their excuse, it's obvious that they fouled up royally."

"True."

"Anybody would understand why you refused to be in their custody."

"True again."

Her gaze searched his face. "If you turn yourself in, you'll be taken to Chicago and sequestered before the trial. After that, you'll probably be in the witness protection program. I might not see you again."

He couldn't resist her any longer. His arm slipped around her waist, and he pulled her against him. "If you want to find me, you will."

"But there are rules."

"Since when did the rules stand in your way?"

She was a fighter, doing what she thought was right in

spite of conventions and restrictions. She'd arranged to spring him from the custody of the marshals.

Her head tilted back. Her lips parted. He kissed her long and hard. They needed to be on the move. Didn't have a moment to spare. Still, he took his time, savoring this moment when her body melted against him. He wanted to make love to her in the soft light of dawn, and he could feel her yearning. She wanted it, too.

He murmured, "Have we known each other long enough?"

"Not yet." She exhaled a sigh. "Soon."

They were meant to be together. He knew it.

Chapter Eighteen

Jack saw only one vehicle outside the safe house: the black SUV with the demolished front end and the flat tires. Since there was no reason for the police to conceal their presence, he assumed no one was here guarding the place. Still, he used caution, parking about a hundred yards away in a forested area and camouflaging their ATV with loose brush.

As they approached the house, Caitlyn said, "They didn't even put up yellow crime scene tape. This doesn't seem right."

"I'm guessing the sheriff has his hands full." Last night, local law enforcement had taken five dangerous men into custody, dealt with the death of U.S. Marshal Hank Perry and started a manhunt. There would be jurisdictional considerations. Not to mention dealing with the media. "I expect they'll call in CSI's from Denver or even from the FBI."

"But shouldn't a deputy be here to make sure people like us don't come in and mess up the scene?"

He didn't sense a trap, but he'd been wrong before. "Let's not question our good luck. We'll get in and out ASAP."

The front door was locked, but enough of the windows had been shot out that it wasn't a problem to shove one open and climb inside. In spite of the devastation caused by last night's firefight, Jack recognized the front room and the adjoining kitchen with pine paneling on two of the walls. He remembered sitting at the table, playing penny-ante poker with the marshals; he had suspected Patterson of cheating.

In the middle of the hallway, he went into the room where he'd been sleeping and turned on the overhead light. Shutters were closed and locked over the only window. The simple furnishings included a single bed, dresser and desk.

"Charming," Caitlyn said sarcastically. "This looks like a pine-paneled prison cell."

"The Marshals Service doesn't use interior decorators. The idea is to keep the witness safe. That's why the windows are shuttered."

"It wouldn't hurt to hang a couple of pictures or stick a ficus in the corner." She went to the desk and pulled open the middle drawer. "What are we looking for?"

"I'd like to find my wallet." He rifled through the dresser. His T-shirts and clothing were bland and familiar, nothing special. "I didn't have time to grab anything when we were under assault."

She held up a paperback book. "Science fiction?"

"I like androids. And don't bother reading anything into that."

"But it's so accurate," she said. "It totally makes sense that you'd be attracted to a human-looking creature with super-abilities and no real emotions."

He had emotions, plenty of them. They pressed at the edge of his peripheral vision like certain blindness. When he had slept in this room, his name was Nick Racine. Pieces of that identity were drawing together, threatening to overwhelm him. "It was a mistake to come here."

"What are you remembering?"

Too much. Not enough. "We should go."

She stepped in front of the door, blocking his retreat. "You can't run away from this. Sooner or later, you'll have to quit using the name of some poor guy who wanted to be my handyman."

She was right, damn it. "Where do I start?"

"With something you remember. Tell me what happened when you were attacked. It was close to midnight, right?"

"Yes." He didn't want to remember.

"You were in bed," she said.

"That's right." He pivoted and went to the unmade bed. In the paneling above the headboard, he spotted six bullet holes in a close pattern, probably fired from a semi-automatic.

"What did you hear?" she asked.

"I was asleep. A noise woke me. The sound of a door slamming or a distant shout. I didn't know exactly what it was, but I got up, pulled on my pants and flannel shirt. Stuck my feet into my boots. Then all hell broke loose. I heard gunfire."

"Did someone come into the room?"

"The door crashed open. Perry shoved me down on the floor. Everything happened fast." The vision inside his head was chaos. Bullets flying. The flash of a knife blade. A burst of pain. "Perry was shot, but he got back up. We made it to the door at the end of the hallway. We were outside. Fighting for our lives."

"What about Patterson and Bryant?"

"Didn't see them. Perry must have told me they deserted us because I was mad." A sudden realization occurred to him. "I didn't have my gun, didn't have time to get my gun."

"Why is that important?" she asked.

He looked down into her bright blue eyes. "You're good at this interviewing stuff."

"It's kind of my job, Jack. And don't change the subject. Why is your gun important?"

"For one thing, I wasn't supposed to be armed. That's not the way witness protection works."

"I don't suppose it is," she said.

"If I hadn't been trying to hide my weapon, I would have slept with the gun beside the bed. Within easy reach." A mistake he'd never make again. "My response would have been faster. Perry wouldn't have died."

He crossed the room. The closet door was open. Hanging inside were a couple of shirts, a jacket and the charcoal-gray suit he intended to wear at the trial. He closed the door, knelt and pulled at the edge of the paneling near the floor. A foot-long section came off in his hand. He had created a cache inside the wall. Inside was a gray flannel bag.

"Very cool," she said. "Those are some serious precautions you took."

He opened the drawstring on the bag, reached inside and removed the Beretta M9. This gun belonged to Nick Racine; it carried a lot of memories. The grip felt like shaking hands with an old friend. His identity was coming back to him.

Something else was in the bag. Through the cloth, he felt a round object that was probably about an inch in diameter. He shook the bag, and it fell onto the floor by his feet. The gleam of silver caught his gaze.

"An earring," Caitlyn said.

Holding the post between his thumb and forefinger, he lifted the earring to eye level. Delicate threads wove a weblike pattern inside the circle. A dream catcher.

He sat on the floor, holding his gun in one hand and the silver earring in the other. Memory overpowered him.

He saw her from afar—lovely as an oasis in the rugged desert terrain. She stood in the open doorway of an adobe house. Her thick, black hair fell in loose curls to her shoulders. When he parked his car and got out, she ran to greet him. The closer she came, the more beautiful she was. Her dark eyes lit from the inside.

She threw herself into his arms. "Oh, Nick. I missed you so much."

He loved this woman. Elena. His wife.

A sob caught in the back of his throat, and he swallowed his sorrow. Oceans of tears wouldn't bring her back. He stared at the earring. "She didn't like jewelry. Rings got in the way when she was working with clay. Necklaces were too fancy. But she wore these earrings. Do you know the legend behind the dream catcher?"

In a quiet voice, Caitlyn said, "The web allows good dreams to filter through and stops the nightmares."

"I gave her these earrings so she'd sleep easy when I wasn't around to protect her." He remembered the silver dream catcher glimmering against her shining black hair. "Nothing could keep her safe. When I found her body, she was wearing only one of these earrings."

It had been his hope to bury her with the earrings, and he'd searched long and hard for the mate to this one. He'd gone through her closet, checked the box of jewelry she never wore, had felt along every inch of floor in the house, and he'd come up empty-handed.

Someone had taken the earring. The murderer.

But the red-haired man didn't have it.

With a sigh, he continued, "I lost them both. My wife and her father, my mentor. It was almost four years ago. I blamed myself for not being there, but Elena wasn't killed because of me. She was staying with her father, and he had enemies."

"Did Rojas kill them?" she asked.

"Someone hired the red-haired man. I wasn't sure who and I needed to know. That's why I created the identity of Tony Perez. Through Santoro, I thought I'd get close enough to the Rojas brothers to find out who was responsible." But he'd failed. The old familiar emptiness spread through him. He didn't care if he lived or died. "That's the life story of Nick Racine."

An identity he never wished to resume.

CAITLYN KNELT BESIDE HIM on the floor with her hands in her lap, itching to reach out to him and hold him. She was there for him, supporting him. If he wanted to talk, she'd listen. If he needed to cry, her shoulder was ready and waiting.

But he didn't reach out. His gaze averted, he withdrew into himself.

She'd seen this reaction from others. No stranger to tragedy, she had experienced the aftermath of violent death while embedded with the troops. Everyone dealt with the pain of sudden loss in their own way, and his grief was deep, intense, almost unimaginable. His wife had been murdered. At the same time, he'd lost his mentor—a man who not only taught him but was his father-in-law.

No wonder Jack had retreated into amnesia. It must have been a relief to shed the burden of being Nick Racine.

He stared at the dream catcher earring. The delicate silver strands contrasted with his rough hands. What was he thinking? What memories haunted him?

From outside, she heard the grating of tires on the gravel driveway. Someone was approaching the safe house.

Though she thought this might be a good time for him to turn himself in, that wasn't her decision to make.

Softly, she spoke his name. "Nick?"

He didn't seem to hear her.

"Nick, there's a car coming."

Immobile, he continued to stare at the memento from his dead wife.

More loudly, she said, "Jack."

He looked at her as though he was seeing her for the first time. He pressed the dream catcher against his lips and slipped it into his pocket. Slowly, he rose to his feet. "We'll see who it is before we decide what to do."

He directed her down the hallway to the rear door, unfastened the lock and stepped outside. She followed as he rounded the house and stopped. From this vantage point, they could see the front of the house.

Jack peeked around the edge. Under his breath, he cursed.

Caitlyn looked past his shoulder and saw Bryant and Patterson emerge from their vehicle. Until now, she and Jack had been riding on a wave of good luck. They'd escaped from the ranch and hidden at Woodley's without anyone coming after them. Apparently, that positive trend had reversed. The two marshals were the last people she wanted to meet.

"What should we do?" She looked to Jack for an answer, but he'd sunk back into a daze of sorrow. He leaned against the wall of the house, staring blankly into the distance.

This apathy didn't work for her. They were in trouble, and she needed for him to be sharp and focused. She needed for him to be Jack.

Bryant took off his cowboy hat and dragged his hand through his hair. "I still don't get it. Why the hell did you make such a big stink about this place being our jurisdiction?"

"Because it is." Patterson dragged his feet. The older man's exhaustion was evident. "This safe house belongs to the U.S. Marshals Service. Besides, I need to keep the CSI's away. When they start prowling around, they'll find clues."

"They're going to figure out what we did, especially when the men they've got in custody start talking."

"Rojas's men? They won't talk. They're too afraid of their boss to make a peep."

"It's over. We ain't going to get out of this." The tall Texan leaned against the side of the vehicle. "I don't want to go to prison, man. I say we make a run for it."

"There's another option."

She watched as Patterson opened the back door of the vehicle and reached inside. Jack had roused himself enough to observe, and she was glad that he'd decided to pay attention.

When Patterson emerged from the car, he held an automatic gun in his hand.

"It's the SIG Sauer," Jack whispered. "Perry's gun."

Jack had also been using that gun. He'd spent all but two bullets defending her when Rojas and his men came after her at her house.

Patterson rounded the front of the car and raised the gun, aiming at the center of Bryant's chest. "Sorry, kid."

The tall Texan turned toward his partner. His back was to them as he held up both hands. "What are you doing?"

"Don't worry. I'm not going to kill you."

"Kill me? What?"

"My God, you're dumb." She saw disgust in Patterson's weary face. "I'm so damned tired of having to explain every tiny detail to you. This is simple. I need to convince our supervisor that Nick Racine went off the rails and is dangerous."

"By shooting me?"

"I'll tell them that Nick shot you," Patterson said. "This gun is proof. Nick used it. When ballistics compares bullets, it proves that he's dangerous."

"Don't do it," Bryant pleaded. "We can go on the run. Rojas will protect us. He'll give us more money and—"

"Shut up," Patterson snapped. "I'm not going into hiding. I have a family. I have a pension. I'm not giving those things up."

Quietly, Jack said, "Patterson can't trust the kid to keep his mouth shut. He's going to kill him."

Apparently, Bryant had come to the same conclusion. He reached for the gun on his belt.

Jack stepped clear of the house, took aim and fired.

His marksmanship was nothing short of amazing. His bullet hit Patterson's arm. He clutched at the wound near his shoulder and staggered backward. The SIG fell from his hand.

Bryant reacted. He whirled, gun in hand, and faced Jack.

"Drop it," Jack said.

The Texan looked back at the partner who had intended to kill him. Then at Jack. Caitlyn could almost see the wheels turning inside his head as he made his decision. *The wrong decision.*

He fired at Jack.

She heard the bullet smack into the house just above her head.

Jack returned fire. Two shots. Two hits.

The Texan fell to the dirt.

Chapter Nineteen

There was a lot of blood, but both marshals were still moving. Not dead. Caitlyn wondered why she wasn't shrinking into the shadows at the side of the house, paralyzed by terror, and then she realized that she wasn't afraid; she trusted Jack to protect her.

Patterson lurched backward and braced himself against the car. With his good arm, he reached across his body toward the gun on his hip.

"Don't try it," Jack warned. "You make one more move, and my next bullet goes through the center of your forehead."

The gray-haired marshal dropped his arm. His left hand was bloody from the wound on his right arm. His dark windbreaker with U.S. Marshal stenciled across the back was slick with gore.

On the ground, Bryant struggled to sit up. His face contorted in pain, and he was groaning, almost sobbing. In his beige jacket, his injuries were more obvious. One of Jack's bullets had ripped through his right shoulder. He'd also been shot in the right thigh. His gun was out of his reach, and he seemed to be suffering too much to go after it.

Caitlyn asked, "What are you going to do with them?"

"First, I'll make sure they're completely disarmed. They're both wearing ankle holsters and probably have a couple of other weapons stashed. Next, I'll get rid of their cell phones."

"Will you kill them?"

"Not unless it's necessary," he said. "I want you to go back to the ATV and wait for me."

Her natural curiosity told her to stay and observe. She wanted to see how Jack got these men to give up their weapons and to hear what they said to each other. By leaving, she'd be walking out before the story was finished.

But she was well aware that she and Jack had no backup. This situation wasn't like anything she'd encountered in the Middle East. Replacement troops weren't going to be riding over the hill to help them out. The smartest thing she could do was to follow Jack's orders. "I'll be waiting."

She jogged around the house and the barn to the forest where they'd hidden the four-wheeler. Was Jack going to finish what he'd started? With her out of the way, would he kill the marshals? She remembered what he'd told her about executing the man who'd murdered his wife. In her frame of reference, an execution meant killing in cold blood. In his identity as Nick Racine, he was a murderer.

But Jack wasn't. Though he didn't hesitate to use physical violence, he hadn't killed anyone. He'd said it wasn't his job. Had he been talking about an occupation? Clearly, he had training in marksmanship, and his hand-to-hand combat skills were finely honed.

At the ATV, she pulled away the brush that camouflaged the vehicle. There was a lot she didn't know about Nick Racine. A lot she needed to find out.

Right now, there was a more pressing issue. By shooting the marshals, Jack had—ironically—given credence to Patterson's plan to discredit him. When the marshals were rescued, they would accuse Jack of ambushing them. Every law-enforcement person involved in the search for Rojas would shift their focus toward Jack. And toward her.

There was no way they could turn themselves in with any guarantee of safety. Not unless she could negotiate the terms with someone she trusted, someone like Danny or Mr. Woodley. She wished she'd kept up with her contacts stateside. At one time, she'd known people in high places. There were still a few. A plan began to form in her mind.

She saw Jack running toward her. Since she hadn't heard any other gunfire, she assumed he hadn't shot Patterson and Bryant. There wasn't any blood on his clothes, so he hadn't knifed them. She might have thought less of him if he'd murdered the marshals, even though they were despicable men who deserved punishment.

He climbed onto the front seat of the ATV. "Let's roll."

"I know exactly which way to go."

Their first challenge would be to get across the main highway without being seen. Since it was early on a Sunday, there wouldn't be much traffic, but law enforcement would be watching the roads. Leaning forward and shouting over the noise of the engine, she directed him to a ridge over-looking a section of road that wasn't fenced. "Stop here."

He killed the engine. "Use your cell phone. Call 911 and get an ambulance out to the safe house."

"Are you sure?"

"I don't like those two morons, but they're still marshals. They must have done something useful in their lives."

As far as she was concerned, that was an awfully generous assumption. Still, she made the call and turned off her phone.

To Jack she said, "You could have killed them."

"That's not who I am."

"Nick Racine?"

He pulled off his helmet and turned in his seat. She studied his face, searching for the terrible sadness that consumed him when he held the silver dream catcher. His expression was grim and as unreadable as granite.

"I've committed murder," he said, "but I'm not a killer. If there's another way, that's the path I'll chose."

"Why?"

"Death is permanent. If you make a mistake, there's no chance for a do-over."

She knew they needed to get moving. There wasn't time for him to answer all the questions that boiled inside her brain. "I want to know about Nick Racine."

Like the sun coming out from behind a cloud, the sexy grin slid onto his face. "Call me Jack."

She answered with a smile of her own. "As if you were born in the moment you walked up to my cabin?"

"Something like that."

What an amazing fantasy! Yesterday morning, the only thought in her mind had been repairing the roof on her barn. She certainly hadn't been thinking about a mate, but if she had imagined the perfect man, he'd be strong, handsome and capable. He'd be complex and interesting. He'd be sexy. He'd be…Jack.

Her heart gave a hard thump against her rib cage. There was no denying her attraction to him. Did it really matter who he was or what he'd done? Fate had dropped him into her life. She was meant to be with him.

She picked up her helmet. "We need to get across the road without anybody seeing us."

"Hang on."

He turned the key in the ignition and maneuvered down the hill. This stretch of road was relatively straight, with good visibility in either direction. There were no other vehicles in sight. The ATV bounced over a ditch, onto the shoulder and across the pavement. It seemed that they'd made it safely across this hurdle, but she wanted to be sure.

"Go into the trees and stop," she said.

He followed her instructions and parked again. He must have been following her line of thinking because he quickly dismounted and moved to a position where he could see the road which was a couple of hundred yards from where they were standing. His gaze scanned from left to right. "We're not being followed."

A beat-up Dodge truck rumbled along the road, traveling a lot faster than the limit. She saw nothing suspicious about his speed; people who lived in the mountains treated the posted limits as guidelines rather than laws.

She heard the wail of an emergency vehicle. As they watched, an ambulance raced past. It was followed by an SUV with the sheriff's logo on the door. In just a few minutes, Patterson would be spewing his lies to the local officers.

"We're in big trouble," she murmured.

His arm encircled her waist. With the thumb of his other hand, he lifted her chin so she was looking up at him. "This might be the right time for you to turn yourself in. After Patterson tells the cops how I went berserk and shot them both, the search is going to get intense. Dangerous."

"I'm pretty sure he's going to implicate me in his lies." She slipped her arm around him. Their bodies had become accustomed to each other; they fit together perfectly. "Besides, you need me. I have a plan that's nothing short of brilliant."

"Brilliant, huh?"

When he combed his fingers through her hair, she realized that her ponytail had come undone. She shook her head. "I must look awful. Do I have helmet hair?"

"Tell me about this plan."

"The way I figure, being taken into custody isn't really the problem. You want to make it to the trial to testify."

"Correct." He kissed the center of her forehead.

"We need to find someone in authority who can facilitate the process and get you to court." Though his kiss distracted her, she kept talking. "I actually do have a contact I can call upon. Someone who knows me and trusts me."

"Who?"

"He's a full-bird colonel, and he's stationed at the Air Force Academy. Once we're on the base, we're under the jurisdiction of the military. Nobody else can touch us, neither the police nor the marshals."

Jack pulled his head back and looked at her with a combination of surprise and appreciation that made her feel warm inside. "How did you get to be so smart?"

"You have your talents," she said, "and I have mine."

"And what makes you think he won't throw us into the brig?"

"He's a fair man," she said. "He'll at least listen to what I have to say. We spent enough time together in the Middle East for him to know that I'm trustworthy."

"Let's contact him and put an end to this. Give him a call on your cell phone."

"I can't really do that. Technically, he doesn't have jurisdiction if we're not on the base. We have to go there. But the Academy isn't that far, only about forty-five miles."

"So all we have to do is make it across forty-five miles through rugged mountain terrain. On a four-wheeler. With deputies, cops, the Marshals Service and the FBI looking for us."

"And possibly Rojas," she said.

He snugged her tightly against him. "Piece of cake."

His kiss was quick and urgent. There wasn't time for

a delicate building of passion; they needed to put miles between themselves and the search parties.

They took their places on the four-wheeler, and he asked, "Any instructions?"

"Keep going in a southeastern direction. Avoid the roads, the fences and cabins."

Turning invisible would have been a handy trick, but neither she nor Jack was magical. To find their way through the mountains, they would have to rely on her sense of direction and her memory.

During the summers when her family stayed at the cabin, she and her brother had taken daylong horse rides to Colorado Springs. Mostly, they'd followed marked trails and roads—an option that she and Jack didn't have. Still, she figured that she wasn't plunging into an altogether unfamiliar wilderness.

Instead of going deeper into the forested area, Jack drove at the edge of the trees, putting distance between them and the safe house. Their route was parallel to a barbed-wire fence with a rugged dirt path beside it. Other four-wheelers probably used that path. Following it would have allowed them to go faster, but she didn't want to risk running into anyone else.

When the distance between the trees and the fence narrowed, Jack veered into the trees. Their progress was slow and bumpy. This vehicle wasn't built for comfort or for long-distance travel. Her already-bruised tailbone ached.

After what seemed like an eternity, Jack found a space without cabins or road and came to a stop. She immediately hopped off, stretched and walked stiffly.

Jack looked up toward the sun. "It's getting close to noon. Do you have any idea where we are?"

"My butt is in hell," she muttered. "All I can say for sure is that we're in the front range of the Rockies."

"A while back, I spotted a road sign. It said something about Roxborough State Park and Sedalia."

"Great," she muttered.

"We've been headed south and mostly east."

"I know."

She'd been pointing him that way. Their route would have been easier if they'd followed South Platte River Road, but she knew there would be fishermen—witnesses who might feel compelled to report a noisy ATV that was scaring the trout.

Jack went to a storage container behind the second seat and opened the lid. "You said Woodley packed some food."

Dear, sweet Mr. Woodley. She hoped he wouldn't be fooled by Patterson's lies, wouldn't think the worst of her. Sooner or later, he'd probably contact her parents. She shuddered to think of what they'd say. Mom hadn't been at all happy when she'd taken the assignment in the Middle East. Now Caitlyn was on the run with a desperate fugitive.

She took out her cell phone. "I should give Mr. Woodley a call."

"Don't turn it on."

She paused with the phone in her hand, watching as he held the quart-size canteen to his lips and took a long glug. He wiped his mouth with the back of his hand and said, "Even if your phone is supposedly untraceable, we can't take a chance. It's likely the FBI is involved in the manhunt. They might have equipment to track the signal."

Morosely, she shoved the phone back into her pocket. "I suppose using the GPS function to get our bearings is out of the question."

He held out a sandwich. "Eat something. It'll make your butt feel better."

Though his logic left a lot to be desired, she took the

food. Her mouth was so dry that she nearly choked, but the ham-and-cheese sandwich tasted good. A hot cup of coffee would have been heaven, but she settled for water.

Jack ate his sandwich in a couple of giant bites and started digging through their supplies. "There are a couple of oranges and bananas. And a whole box of energy bars. What is it with you mountain people and granola?"

"Easy to carry and yummy to eat. Give me one."

After taking in food and water, she felt immeasurably better—nearly human, in fact. When Jack suggested hiking to the top of the rise to get their bearings, she was ready. Any activity that didn't involve sitting sounded good.

Her muscles stretched as she hiked. She swung her arms and wiggled her hips. Walking the rest of the way to the Air Force Academy seemed preferable to more hours on the back of the ATV.

She joined Jack on the rocky crest devoid of trees. The wind brushed through the tangles in her hair, which undoubtedly resembled a bird's nest, but she didn't care. An incredible panorama filled her vision and gave her strength. In the distance, she saw Pike's Peak, capped with snow.

Energizing her body seemed to help her brain. As she gazed across the rugged landscape, she knew where they were and where they should be headed. She pointed. "We go that way."

"Any particular reason why?"

"The best place to hide is in plain sight," she said. "We're close to the Rampart Range Recreational Area. It's full of trails that are sanctioned for ATVs. With our helmets, we'll blend in with the other off-roaders."

He didn't answer immediately. Preoccupied, he stared into the sky. "I see a chopper."

"And there will be a lot more planes and gliders and

such as we get closer to the Academy. It's nothing to worry about."

"You're probably right." He shrugged but still looked worried. "I like your plan. If we're on a trail, we can move faster."

"Okay," she said. "Let's hit the road, Jack."

He raised an eyebrow. "How long have you been waiting to say that?"

"Hours."

Not all of her thinking was about escape. Sometimes, they just needed a chuckle.

Chapter Twenty

Though Jack made several more rest stops in the afternoon, the constant vibration of the four-wheeler was getting to him. Navigating this machine through the wilderness was like crashing through a maze on a bucking bronco.

When they found the groomed trails of the Rampart Range Recreational Area, the ride was a hundred times smoother. In comparison to open terrain, these trails were like cruising on polished marble. Finally, they were getting somewhere. Approaching the last step in their journey.

As soon as he was taken into custody by Caitlyn's colonel, he'd be swept into the system and transported to Chicago to testify. His time with her would be over. Sure, they'd promise to see each other again after the trial. They'd make plans. Maybe even meet for coffee. But she'd be charging back into her career. And he'd likely be in witness protection.

He didn't want to lose her.

Other ATVs and dirt bikes buzzed along the trails around them, careening around sharp turns and flying over bumps in the road. Woodley's four-wheeler was more utilitarian than recreational, not designed for stunts. Their top speed was about forty or forty-five, and Jack was moving considerably slower.

A skinny teenager in a flame helmet zipped past them and shouted, "Step on it, Grandpa."

"I'll step on you," he muttered. He cranked the accelerator. Then he backed off. This was no time for a motocross race.

At a fork in the trail, he stopped at a carved wooden marker with arrows pointing the way to different trails. Behind him, Caitlyn was quick to choose. "Left," she said. "It's a camping area."

He didn't much care for organized campsites; having other people around ruined the experience. "What if we have to register? Neither of us have wallets or IDs."

"We don't have to stay there," she said. "But we can fill our water bottle. And maybe there's a bathroom. Oh, God, I'd love to find a bathroom. Even an outhouse."

A half mile down the trail was a large camping area with several separate sites, two of which were occupied by other ATV riders. Their campfires tinted the air with pungent smoke. His concern about registering was unfounded. There wasn't a ranger station, just a couple of restrooms in a small house designed to look like a log cabin. He parked behind the restrooms and watched as Caitlyn went inside.

He stood for a minute and waited before he decided it wasn't necessary to stand guard. If anyone had been following them, they'd have made their move long before now. He glanced around the area. *Were they safe?* More than once, he'd seen choppers swooping like giant dragonflies across the skies. *Aerial surveillance?* It was possible. But the helicopters hadn't come closer or hovered above them.

He took his helmet with him as he strolled through the groomed area surrounded by a thick forest of lodgepole pine and Douglas fir. This land had been untouched by wildfires, and the foliage grew in robust clumps. A narrow creek trickled beyond the edge of the campground. He stood beside it and listened to the sound of rippling water mingled with the distant voices of the other campers.

The late afternoon sunlight reflected on the water as it rushed to join with a wider river or a lake or, perhaps, to flow all the way to the Gulf of Mexico. Everything had a destination. Every person had a future, even a man with no past.

He used to be Nick Racine. Not anymore. Though the full picture of his past was hazy, he vividly remembered the soul-deep devastation after Elena's murder. The single earring in his pocket reminded him of broken dreams—a future he'd lost. Tragedy had consumed him. Then rage. Then he'd embarked on the quest for revenge that turned him into a murderer.

When amnesia wiped the slate clean, he was freed from his past. He didn't know what fate had directed him to Caitlyn's cabin, but he was grateful. She had refused to give up on him. She'd believed in him. Literally, she knew Jack Dalton better than anyone else.

She came up beside him. "I found a brochure in a box at the bathroom. There's a trail map."

The squiggly lines marking the trails resembled a tangle of yarn, but he zoomed in on the important part. "Here's where we come out. Woodland Park."

"From there, it's a straight shot to the back entrance to the Air Force Academy," she said. "We're close. But it's late. I think we should stop for the night."

It wasn't necessary to stop. Their vehicle had headlights, and Jack knew he could push his endurance and reach the Academy tonight. But he was in favor of camping tonight; he didn't want his time with her to end. He pointed to a location on the map. "We'll camp here."

She squinted to read the tiny name beside the dot. "Devil's Spike? The code says there's no bathroom or water."

"It's not far from here. Looks like a couple of squiggly miles up the road we're on."

"Why can't we stay right here?"

"Witnesses," he said.

He turned on his heel and walked back to the four-wheeler. His reason for choosing the most remote location on the map was simple: he wanted to be alone, completely alone, with her.

Grumbling, she climbed onto the back of the ATV. In less than fifteen minutes, they'd climbed a zigzag trail to the Devil's Spike area. Each campsite consisted of a cleared space, a table and a fire ring. Each was separated from the others by trees and rocks. All were deserted. It was Sunday night, not a time when many people were camping.

While Caitlyn climbed onto the top of the wood picnic table and sat with her feet on the bench, he took the sleeping bags from the storage container. Since they didn't have a tent or any other gear, setting up camp was simply a matter of spreading the bags on the flattest part of the clearing.

He took the freshly filled water bottle and joined her on the table. Devil's Spike was higher than the other campground. From this vantage point, they overlooked rolling hills covered with trees and dotted with jagged rock formations—one of which was probably supposed to be the Spike. In the west, the sun had begun to set, coloring the sky a brilliant magenta and gilding the underbellies of clouds with molten gold.

For a change, Caitlyn was quiet. And so was he.

After spending the entire day with the roar of the ATV motor, the stillness of the mountains was a relief. The wind was cool enough to be refreshing without making him shiver.

He gazed toward her. The glow of the sunset touched her cheekbones and picked out strands of gold in her hair. He'd told her several times that she was smart, tough and brave, but he'd forgotten the most important thing. She was a beautiful woman.

She exhaled a sigh and stretched, rotating her shoulders and turning her head from side to side.

"Sore?" he asked.

"From my toes to the top of my head. My butt is killing me."

"I've got a cure." He brushed the twigs and pine cones from the surface of the table. "Lie down. I'll give you a massage."

She hesitated for a nanosecond before stripping off her jacket, which she folded into a makeshift pillow. She lay down on her stomach on the table. "Be gentle," she said. "I'm not a big fan of the deep tissue stuff."

He started by lightly kneading the tense muscles of her shoulders and neck. The fabric of her T-shirt bunched under his fingers. "You really should be nude."

"If I was naked on this table, I'd come away with a belly full of splinters."

He stroked lower on her back. He could count her ribs, but her body was soft and feminine, with a slim waist and a sensual flare of her hips. *Really beautiful.* He needed to tell her.

When he returned to her shoulders, she gave a soft moan—the kind of sound that lovers made. For several minutes, he continued to massage, and her moans got deeper and more sensual. "Oh, Jack. That's amazing."

He agreed. It felt pretty damned good to him, too.

As he rubbed near her tailbone, she tensed. "Be careful, that hurts."

"Let me take a look."

Before she could object, he reached around to unbutton her jeans. He slid the denim down her hips. A patch of black and blue colored the milky skin above her bottom.

She grumbled, "Are you staring at my butt?"

"You've got a nice little bruise back here."

"Really?" She twisted her torso, trying to look over her shoulder. "Where?"

"Without a mirror, you aren't going to be able to see it."

"Are you sure it's bruised?"

"How does this feel?" With two fingers, he pressed against bruise.

"Hurts," she said. "What should I do about it?"

"I could kiss it and make it better."

She rolled onto her back and looked up at him. Her eyes were the purest blue he'd ever seen. Now was the time to give her his sincere compliments about her beauty, but he found himself tongue-tied. What the hell was wrong with him? He wasn't inexperienced with women, but this felt like his first time.

"There's something," he blurted, "something I need to say."

Her eyebrows pulled down. "What is it?"

He couldn't blame her for being worried. Every time she turned around, he threw some giant revelation at her. She probably though he was going to confess to the crime of the century. "It's nothing bad."

"Okay," she said hesitantly.

"I wanted you to know that I appreciate you." *Real smooth, Jack.*

"And I appreciate you, too."

They sounded less intimate than coworkers discussing a business project. He took a breath and started over. "I like the way your hair slips out of the ponytail and falls across your cheek. And the way you squint when you're thinking. And the little gasping noise you make when you laugh."

"I don't snort," she said.

"You catch your breath, as though laughter surprises you. It's a happy sound." Feeling more confident, he glided his hand along her arm. "I like the proportion of your shoulders and your hips. And your long legs. What I'm trying to say is that you're beautiful, Caitlyn."

She reached up and touched his cheek. "Last night, I didn't think we'd known each other long enough to make love."

"And now?"

"It's time."

That was all he needed to hear. He kissed the smile from her lips.

FINALLY! HE WAS KISSING HER. Caitlyn clung to him. His massage had lit her fuse, and she was certain that she'd explode into a million pieces if they didn't make love now, right now.

She expected Jack to show his passion with the same skill he showed in every other physical activity, but he had seemed unsure of himself. His clumsiness was endearing, but not what she was looking for. She wanted him to sweep her off her feet.

As he deepened the kiss, she felt his attitude change. He went from boyish to manly. Dominating and powerful, he took charge. With a surge of strength, he yanked her off the picnic table.

"You're so damn beautiful," he said.

"So are you."

"Men aren't."

"You are."

He carried her across the clearing. She knew he wouldn't stumble or drop her; she trusted him. In his arms, she felt completely safe.

His step was sure as he bent his legs and lowered her onto the smooth fabric of the sleeping bag on the ground. Not exactly a feather bed, but she was accustomed to sleeping in rough conditions.

Impatient, she tried to pull him down on top of her, but he sat back on his heels. Twilight wrapped around him. His eyes glistened as he consumed her with a gaze. Then he went to her feet and removed her shoes and socks.

She looked down the length of her body, watching him as he stroked her instep and pressed on her toes. Another massage. Incredible! Most men required hours of pleading before they'd rub your feet. A burst of sensual tremors slithered up her legs, rising from her bare feet to her groin. She exhaled a low moan of sheer pleasure.

He moved up her body to her already unfastened jeans. His hand slid inside her waistband. Her thighs spread, welcoming his touch. Quivering in anticipation, she arched her back, inadvertently putting pressure on her bruised tailbone. Pain shot through her. "Ouch."

He stopped what he was doing and stretched out beside her. "Does it hurt?"

"Yes, but I don't want to stop."

"There's only one thing to do." He held her tightly and flipped onto his back. The move was so unexpected that she gasped. She loved the way he manhandled her.

"I get it," she said. "I have to be on top."

She liked this plan. As they undressed each other, she felt like she had some control. She decided the moment when their bare flesh would make contact. Lying naked on top of him, she reveled in the head-to-toe sensation. The cool mountain breeze that flowed down her spine contrasted the heat generated by their joined bodies.

Even though Jack was on the bottom, he remained the aggressor. He directed her with gentle shifts in position and not-so-subtle touches. Her thighs spread. As she straddled him, he moved her hips up and down, rubbing hard.

They were both breathless when he said, "You know I don't have a condom."

"I'm on the pill." Though she craved him, she hesitated. In his life as Racine and as Perez the mob enforcer, he'd been exposed to a lot of bad things. "Do you have any issues I should know about?"

"I'm clean. Haven't made love since I was in the hospital."

Her fingers ran along the edge of the scar on his torso. "You were Tony Perez when you were shot."

"A lifetime ago."

When he pulled her against his body, she knew that one night with him wasn't enough. She couldn't imagine a lifetime without Jack.

Chapter Twenty-One

Caitlyn had been right to assume that Jack would be a great lover. He knew all the right moves and some unusual twists that had surprised and delighted her. Their first bout of lovemaking had been fierce and hungry. The second time was more about gentleness and finesse.

On her side, she curled up inside the sleeping bags they'd zipped together. No other campers had chosen Devil's Spike, and she was glad for the privacy as she watched Jack—naked except for his boots—as he started a fire in the rock-lined pit.

Though she was enjoying the show, she said, "We don't really need a fire. We don't have anything to cook."

Crouched in the darkness, he coaxed the flames. "It's a primal thing. Like a caveman."

His long, lean body was far too sculpted to be that of a primitive man. She'd told him that he was beautiful, and she'd meant it. He reminded her of a perfect sculpture.

"We don't need the fire for warmth," she said. The early summer night was chilly, but the thermal sleeping bag would keep them warm enough.

He stepped away from the pit and looked down on the tiny dancing flames. "Call it ambience. Or protection from bears. Every campsite needs a fire."

When he crawled into the sleeping bag beside her, his

skin was cold. It took a couple minute of giggling and wrestling for them both to get comfortable. They ended up in a spooning position, facing the fire with his arms snuggled around her.

Turning her head, she looked up through the tracery of pine boughs into a brilliant, starry night. She should have been perfectly content, but the wheels in the back of her mind had started turning. She was thinking about tomorrow. Turning to the colonel for help was the right thing to do, and she was sure he'd get Jack where he needed to be for the trial. And then what would happen?

As a journalist, she could use her press credentials to stay in touch with him until she'd written her story. But she couldn't violate the rules of witness protection to be with him unless she was willing to give up her own identity and disappear. She couldn't do that, couldn't sever her ties with her family and friends. The most important thing she'd learned from this experience was the value of friendship. She and Jack never would have escaped if it hadn't been for Heather, Danny and Mr. Woodley.

"After you testify," she said, "do you have to go into the WitSec program?"

"I was wondering how long it would take."

"How long what would take?"

He nuzzled her ear. "Until you started asking questions again."

"I don't want to say goodbye to you tomorrow." They had forged a bond, made a connection unlike anything she'd ever known. She might actually be falling in love with him. "We need to spend more time together."

"I wonder how much money I have."

"What?" She wriggled around until she was facing him. "What are you thinking?"

"When I was Nick Racine, I wonder if I was rich or poor or somewhere in between."

They hadn't had much luck researching his finances or his identity on the computer. "I couldn't find Nick Racine in any of the usual credit databases. Online, you don't exist."

"Which brings up a couple of possibilities," he said. "I might be someone who lived completely off the grid. Or I might have a numbered Swiss bank account."

"Those are the choices? Either you were a criminal or a mogul?"

"I vote for mogul. Then I wouldn't have to worry about WitSec. I'd buy an island in the tropics with a waterfall, and we could live there, eating coconuts and mangos."

"Not the best location for a reporter," she said.

"You'd adjust, and I'd buy you a newspaper of your own. *The Caitlyn Daily News*." With the firelight glimmering in his tousled black hair, he was disconcertingly gorgeous.

"Unfortunately, we don't know if you're a crook or a billionaire. We need more information. Seems like we're back to the beginning. We need to know more about your past."

"Blank," he said. "Not being able to remember isn't entirely due to amnesia. I consciously erased Nick Racine. Couldn't live with the tragedy. Or with the way I handled my revenge."

She was tired and hungry. Having him naked beside her made her want to spend the rest of the night making love. But this was important; the future depended on it. "Let's try to figure out the easy stuff. Like your occupation."

"Nothing comes to mind."

With the tip of her finger, she traced the jagged scar from his bullet wound. Other injuries had left their marks on his body. Obviously, he'd lived a physically active, dangerous life. "I think we can rule out Sunday school teacher and peace activist."

"I could be a peace activist," he protested. "I have a gentle side. I like flowers."

"Flowers, huh?" She supposed that any memory was good. "What kind of flowers?"

"Orchids." His sexy grin slid into place. "That's a good sign, right? Orchids are expensive."

He was the furthest thing from a hothouse flower that she could imagine. "Let's go with your skills. What kind of work requires you to be a marksman? Why would you be trained in hand-to-hand combat?"

"The military," he said, "but that doesn't fit. I have no memory of basic training or being on a base, can't imagine myself in a uniform. Besides, you checked military data and didn't find a record of Nick Racine."

Some jobs in the military weren't part of the records. He could have been trained in a special operation—the kind that didn't leave a paper trail. Or he could have been working for an outside organization. "You might be a mercenary."

"Maybe."

She'd never interviewed a mercenary but had met a few. They were cruel, emotionless men with cold eyes and even colder hearts. "You have the skills but not the temperament. If you were a mercenary, you would have slit the throats of Rojas's men at the safe house."

"That's not how I roll." He caressed the line of her throat. "I'm a lover, not a fighter."

She caught his hand. "You're both."

"There's no point in figuring out my past. Tomorrow, when I turn myself in, the federal prosecutors in charge of the trial in Chicago will fill in the blanks. I'm sure they have a fat dossier on Nick Racine and Tony Perez." He raised their hands to his lips and brushed a kiss on her knuckles. "On Tuesday, I'll testify."

She hated this neat, logical package. "What about me? What happens to us?"

"I won't let you go." Though he spoke softly, his voice rang with determination. "Before I met you and became Jack Dalton, I didn't give a damn about my future. I was empty. Didn't care if I lived or died. You changed that."

She'd never been anyone's reason for living. Unexpected tears welled up behind her eyelids. "What next?"

"The possibilities are endless, babe."

A tear slipped down her cheek, and he kissed it away. She never wanted him to leave. She wouldn't say goodbye to him. No matter what.

THE NEXT MORNING, Jack studied the trail map to find the most direct route to Woodland Park. The ATV was running low on fuel, and he didn't want their plan to be derailed by something as mundane as running out of gas.

His focus was clear. He wanted to get this thing over with so he could start his new life. No longer consumed by his past, he was ready for the future.

Caitlyn sat gingerly on the backseat of the four-wheeler. "Know what I want?"

He draped an arm around her shoulder and gave her a quick but thorough kiss. "Some of this?"

She glided her hand down his chest and tugged on the waistband of his jeans. With a grin, she released the fabric and patted his gut. "I really, really want steak and eggs. A medium-rare T-bone. And hash browns."

"When we get to the Academy, I'm sure your colonel friend can arrange it."

"I'm starved." She put on her helmet. "I burned off a lot of calories last night."

"It was a good workout." Their lovemaking hadn't been overly athletic but it had been sustained. He couldn't get enough of her, and he was pretty sure that feeling went both ways. "A lot more fun than when I was training for the triathlon."

She whipped her helmet off and stared at him. "You were in a triathlon?"

He remembered swimming, biking and running with the sun blistering down on his head and shoulders. "My goal was to finish in the top twenty."

"Did you?"

"Sixteenth."

"This is a positive sign, Jack. Your memories are falling back into place."

He wasn't sure how much he wanted to remember. The triathlon had been a proud achievement, but he couldn't help thinking that something in his past would come between them. "It's good to know I don't have permanent brain damage."

When he mounted the ATV and drove away from their campsite, the fuel gauge dipped into the reserve tank. How many more miles did they have before it died? Caitlyn had told him that Woodland Park was only ten miles from the Academy, but she'd been iffy on distances.

The trails were clearly marked, and it didn't take long to find the main road—the most direct route. Barely two lanes, the graded dirt had the reddish color of sandstone. There wasn't much traffic, but the vehicles varied from dirt bikes and ATVs to regular two-wheel drive cars. When a slick, cherry-red, top-down Jeep Wrangler passed them, he watched with envy. The Jeep was a nice ride that made sense on this scenic road. In contrast, Woodley's utilitarian ATV was like driving a lawn mower; it would be virtually useless in a chase.

Being around other vehicles reminded him that they weren't on a pleasure outing. He and Caitlyn were still the center of a manhunt. Last night, he'd felt safer. Nobody could have tracked their bizarre cross-country route from Pinedale.

Today was different. On this road, they weren't hidden by forest. They could be picked out in aerial surveillance. Patterson had talked about hitching a ride on a helicopter. What if that chopper stayed around? What if the marshals had an eye in the sky?

The dirt road snaked along the side of a mountain. Every twisting turn revealed another panorama. At a high point, he pulled onto the shoulder and stopped.

"Something wrong?" Caitlyn asked.

"Not yet."

He walked to the edge of the cliff. In the distance was Pike's Peak, glistening in the morning sunshine. A ribbon of road twisted through the trees below them.

"Nobody can recognize us in our helmets," she said.

It was in his nature to plan for the worst possible outcome. If they were pursued, the dramatic views on a high road without a guardrail would turn into a death trap. Too easily, they could be forced over the edge.

A dark SUV whipped along the road below them. The driver was going too fast, kicking up swirls of dust when he skidded onto the shoulder. "What does that car make you think of?"

"The black SUV," she said. "Rojas."

Gregorio Rojas was wealthy enough to pay for his own aerial surveillance. One of those choppers or gliders had been looking for them, and Rojas himself had come to finish the job.

He climbed onto the ATV and maneuvered if off the road where he hid behind a fat boulder. He and Caitlyn removed their helmets and waited. His Beretta was in his hand.

The SUV zoomed past their hiding place. Its dark-tinted windows made it impossible to see who was inside, but the passengers in this car weren't taking the time to enjoy the mountain scenery.

"They're going too fast," Caitlyn said. "If they meet anybody on this narrow road, they're going to scare the hell out of them."

"Or force them off the road," he said. "And the people they want to meet are us."

"How did they find us?"

"By now the sheriff has probably figured out how we escaped from the ranch. They'll know we took Woodley's four-wheeler. Aerial surveillance will be looking for a two-seat ATV ridden by people in bright blue helmets."

"But how does Rojas know?"

"Patterson." The marshal would have told his lies about how Jack attacked them and shot them. Patterson would still be in the law enforcement loop. "He's feeding information to Rojas."

Any doubt Jack might have had about who was in the SUV vanished when the car came roaring back down the road in the opposite direction. Rojas was searching for them, pinpointing their position. And he wasn't known for leaving survivors.

Chapter Twenty-Two

Jack knew he'd been in similar situations when he was on the run. Memories flashed: hiding in a dry ravine waiting for the sun to set, being chased across a rooftop in San Diego, jumping from an overpass onto a ledge.

In each memory he was alone. The only life he'd risked was his own. He refused to put Caitlyn in danger.

"We can't outrun them in the four-wheeler," he said.

"Do we keep going on foot?"

"Not safe. They'll be armed with sniper rifles. As soon as they spot us, we're dead."

She took out her cell phone. "We need reinforcements. I'm calling the colonel at the Academy."

"What are you going to tell him?"

"The truth," she said. "I'm in danger, and I need his help."

It couldn't hurt to have backup on the way, but Jack needed to do something now. He had to level the playing field. That meant disabling the SUV. Shooting the tires with a handgun was nearly impossible, even for him. But he had to try.

As they watched from their hiding place, the SUV drove past again, moving more slowly this time. At the wide end of the road where he'd pulled off, they turned and went back up the hill and disappeared behind a curve.

"I want you to stay hidden," he said. "If anything happens to me, run."

"Forget it. I'm not leaving you."

He gazed into her clear blue eyes. She'd come a long way from being the woman who froze in terror, but she didn't have his experience or skill. "They're not after you. Rojas wants me dead so I can't testify against his brother."

"But we're a team." Her chin jutted stubbornly. "There's got to be something I can do to help."

"Survive," he said. "That's what I ask of you, Caitlyn. I need for you to get through this in one piece."

"Without you?"

There were worse things than death.

"I lost my wife," he said. "If anything happened to you, I might as well hang it up. I couldn't live with the pain, can't bear to lose another woman I love."

CAITLYN HEARD THE WORDS, but it took a moment for them to sink in. *He loved her.*

She'd been telling herself that she was with him because he was a good story, but she'd violated the cardinal rule of journalism by getting involved with her subject. Involved? Wasn't that a mild way of describing their mind-blowing sex last night? She gave up the pretense. When it came to Jack, she wasn't objective.

"I love you, too."

His sexy grin mesmerized her. "This is going to work out, babe. You stay hidden. Stay safe."

He turned away from her and grabbed his helmet. In a crouch, he dodged through the trees and rocks.

She still held her cell phone, but she couldn't make the call until she knew what Jack was doing. Being careful to stay where she couldn't be seen from the road, she moved to a position beside a tall boulder. Peering through the trunks of trees, she caught a glimpse of his khaki jacket before he ducked behind a shrub at the edge of the cliff where the road made a sharp, hairpin curve.

She saw the SUV coming down the hill toward him.

Many of the people she'd interviewed over the years had told her that the moments before a disaster were so intense that everything happened in slow motion. She'd never experienced that sensation until now. The SUV with dark-tinted windows seemed to be creeping forward an inch at a time.

As she watched, Jack rose from his hiding place. On the edge of the cliff, he stood straight and tall. A gust of wind blew his jacket open. She thought she could see his jaw clench as he raised his gun and sighted down the barrel.

The windows on the SUV descended. A man leaned from the passenger seat. Rojas himself? He had a gun.

A scream crawled up the back of her throat, and she pressed her hands over her mouth to keep from making a noise. *Oh, God. Jack, what are you doing?*

The SUV lurched forward, coming at Jack.

The driver would be forced to turn. If he tried to hit Jack, the car would fly over the edge of the cliff.

She heard two gunshots.

The windshield cracked, but the car kept coming.

The front grille was only a few feet away from Jack. He fired again and again with both hands bracing his gun.

He dived out of the way as the big vehicle swerved into a turn. It was sideways on the corner of the road when the front tire slipped over the loose gravel on the shoulder. Off balance, the car flipped onto its side as it plummeted over the edge.

"Jack." She screamed his name. "Jack, are you all right?"

She couldn't see him.

CLINGING TO THE TRUNK of a scraggly little pine to keep from sliding down the steep incline, Jack ducked his head to avoid the flying shards of rock. A few feet from him, the SUV crashed down the cliff on its side. The drop was close to vertical for about sixty feet. Then the vehicle smashed into an outcropping of rock. Forward momentum flipped the SUV onto the roof, and it slid. The terrain leveled out, but the SUV kept going until it plowed into two tall pine trees.

The upper branches of the trees trembled. Dirt churned in the air. In the aftermath, there was silence, swirling dust and the stink of gasoline.

With his Beretta in his hand, Jack climbed down the craggy rocks toward the SUV that had come to rest upside down.

Nothing moved. The roof was caved in but not flattened. Rojas could have survived. Even if he was injured, he'd shoot to kill.

Keeping his distance, Jack watched and waited.

"Jack!"

Looking up, he saw Caitlyn standing at the top of the cliff. She looked like an angel—a very worried angel.

Waving, he called to her. "I'm all right. Stay where you are."

But she was already climbing over the ledge.

An arm thrust through the open passenger window of the SUV. Rojas clawed his way forward until he was halfway out. One side of his face was raw and bloody. His right arm twisted at an unnatural angle. "Help me."

"Throw out your guns," Jack said.

"Get me out of here. Before the damn car explodes."

"Where's your driver?"

"Dead. His neck broke. Dead." Rojas dragged himself forward an inch at a time. His hips were through the window. "I know it's you. Nick Racine. You son of a bitch."

Jack approached, keeping his Beretta aimed at Rojas, not taking any chances. A wounded man could be dangerous; he had nothing to lose.

Rojas hauled himself free of the car. His left leg, like his arm, was in bad shape. Breathing hard, he rolled onto his back. His face screwed into a knot, fighting the pain.

As far as Jack could tell, he was unarmed.

Caitlyn was all the way down the hill. Not taking his eyes off his enemy, Jack said to her, "Don't come any closer."

"Ambulance," Rojas said. "Get me an ambulance."

"I have my phone," she said.

"Make the 911 call." Jack stood over the injured man. "Make one false move, and I'll shoot."

Rojas glared up with pure hatred in his dark eyes. Deep abrasions had shredded the right side of his face. "You wanted to ruin my family. You and the other damned feds."

What other feds? "Who?"

"DEA."

That was the answer that had eluded him. Three little letters: DEA. In his mind he saw his badge and his official identification papers. He was a DEA agent, an officer of the law. Huge chunks of memory fell into place.

"Bastard." Rojas turned his head and spat. "You sent my brother to jail. You tried to destroy me."

"That's what happens when you're running a drug cartel. You get caught."

With his good hand, Rojas reached into his jacket pocket.

Jack tensed, ready to shoot.

Rojas withdrew a fist. He held his arm toward Jack and opened his hand. "I still win."

In his bloody hand he held a delicate silver dream catcher, the mate of the one Jack had found at the safe house. That earring was as good as a confession. Rojas was responsible for Elena's murder; he had hired the hit man.

Jack stood and aimed his gun at the center of Rojas's chest. If any man deserved killing, it was him. "Why?"

"Her papa was my enemy." His eyelids closed. "Didn't know she was your woman. But I'm glad."

"Rot in hell." He could have pulled the trigger, but it would be more painful for Rojas to survive. He took the earring from the unconscious man's hand, turned his back and walked toward Caitlyn.

She ran to him and threw herself into his arms. "Never do anything like that again. Never."

"I can't make that promise."

She stepped back. Her eyes filled with questions, but she said, "We'd better hurry. I called for an ambulance. That means the police will be here any minute."

"We don't have to run anymore. I remembered. Everything." He took a breath, accepting his identity. "I'm a DEA agent. Most of my work is undercover. I was taught by Elena's father, based in Arizona."

"DEA?" She cocked her head to one side. "You're an undercover agent?"

"That's why I don't have a presence on the internet. I have to keep my identity hidden. It's also how I knew how to turn myself into Tony Perez."

"It's also how you became Jack Dalton."

He didn't want her to think that she was nothing more than another project. "I haven't lied to you. Okay, I did at first when I claimed somebody else's identity. But after that I've told you as much of the truth as I could remember."

"It fits," she said. "When the marshals nearly found us in the cave, they said something about backup. Why didn't you call the DEA for backup?"

"If it hadn't been for the amnesia, I could have contacted my superiors. We wouldn't have gone through all this. Listen, Caitlyn, I'm sorry for scaring the hell out of you. Sorry I put you in danger. Sorry I dragged your friends into this mess. But there's a silver lining."

She gazed past his shoulder to the wreckage of the SUV. "There is?"

He took her hand. "I fell in love with you."

Her lips pinched together. "Is that Jack Dalton talking? Or Nick Racine?"

"Does it matter? They're all me."

Her eyes grew brighter. "Does this mean you won't have to go into witness protection after you testify?"

"If I remember correctly, the agreement I made with the federal prosecutors has me testifying in closed court as Tony Perez. After the trial, Tony disappears. And I go back to my life."

"We can be together?"

"That's right." He caught hold of her hand and pulled her into an easy embrace. "We're together. Until you get sick of me."

"Not going to happen." She rested her head on his chest. "No way can I leave you before I have my Pulitzer-winning story written. It just keeps getting better and better. I start out with the story of a federal witness on the run, and then you turn out to be an undercover agent with amnesia."

His heart sank. This was going to be an obstacle. "You can't write this story."

NO MATTER HOW MANY times he explained it to her, Caitlyn still didn't understand. In the hangar of the small airport where they were waiting for the private jet that would take Jack to Chicago, she paced back and forth in front of him.

"What if I don't use your real name or any of your aliases?"

"You'd still be in danger." He shifted on the worn leather sofa that was pushed up against the metal wall of the hangar. "People who have a problem with me—cartels like Rojas—would know they could find me through you."

She flung herself onto the sofa beside him. Though she would have preferred having this conversation in private, he had two marshals and another DEA agent keeping an eye on him. They stood in a clump by the open door of the hangar. All of them wore sunglasses. All of them were armed.

Her time with Jack was limited. The plane had already landed and was taxiing toward the hangar.

"What happens," she asked, "when we're together and somebody wants to know what you do for a living?"

"Tell them I'm a Sunday school teacher. Or an independently wealthy mogul."

"Even my friends?"

"Especially your friends."

"I hate this." Her life as a journalist was based on ferreting out the truth. How could she live a lie?

He leaned forward, resting his elbows on his knees. "There is a solution. You could have your story published under someone else's name."

"Then who's going to pick up my Pulitzer?"

The main purpose of writing this story was to reestablish herself as an investigative reporter. If she gave the writing credit to someone else, she'd be back to zero. "I have a better idea. You could quit your job."

He shook his head. "I'm pretty good at what I do."

"So am I."

She'd never anticipated this kind of impasse. Before she got involved with Jack, her main project was fixing the roof on the barn. She'd been thinking about giving up her career. It was his belief in her that reminded her how much she loved being a journalist. She couldn't turn her back on a story like this.

The DEA agent approached them. "Time to go."

"Give me a minute," Jack said.

They both stood, and she looked up at him. "You know, I could just write the story, anyway."

"That's your choice."

Her decision was clear. She could be with him and live a lie. Or she could write her story and say goodbye. "I want both."

He rested his hands on her shoulders and gave her a quick kiss. "I hope I'll see you when the trial is over."

As she watched him walk away, her vision blurred with tears. Love wasn't supposed to be this hard.

Chapter Twenty-Three

Nick Racine, aka Tony Perez, was under close protection for the two-week duration of the Rojas trial in Chicago. No phone calls. No emails. No meetings. If he'd insisted, he could have made some kind of arrangement to contact Caitlyn, but he wanted to give her space.

He missed her. It wasn't the same kind of devastating pain he'd felt after Elena's murder. Caitlyn's absence was a gnawing ache that grew sharper with every hour they were apart. There was so much he wanted to tell her, so many things he'd learned about himself.

His childhood was something he never wanted to clearly remember. An alcoholic father. A mother who deserted him. And years in foster care. The only positive was that he'd learned how to fight at an early age.

His financial situation didn't elevate him to mogul status, but he was well-set. He didn't own property, but he did have a numbered Swiss bank account in a different name.

There were dozens of identities he'd used, but the only person he wanted to be was Jack Dalton, the man who was loved by Caitlyn Morris.

At the Federal Courthouse in Chicago, he waited in the hallway outside the courtroom where the trail had taken place. The jury had finished their deliberations.

As a witness, he wasn't allowed inside the room where

he could see the look on Tom Rojas's face, but he wanted to know the verdict as soon as it was announced. Gregorio Rojas hadn't survived the car crash. If his brother was found guilty, the cartel was dead. Jack's revenge was complete.

Mentally, he corrected himself. Nick Racine had lived for revenge and allowed his grief to poison his life. As Jack, he had much more to live for. The future was within his grasp. He just had to make Caitlyn see things his way.

He sensed her presence and turned his head. There she was, striding confidently down the hallway toward him. Her newly trimmed blond hair fell to her shoulders in a smooth curtain. The skirt on her white linen suit was short enough to be interesting. Her high heels were red.

He stood to meet her, and when she stopped a few feet away from him, he was itching to yank her into his arms, to mess up her coiffed hair and kiss the lipstick off her mouth.

With a grin, he said, "You clean up good."

"So do you." She reached toward him and glided her fingers along the lapel of his jacket. "A designer suit."

"It turns out that I've got good taste."

"I knew that. After all, you like me."

Having her this close was driving him crazy. She was everything he wanted. "The way I feel about you goes a lot deeper than liking."

The door to the courtroom swung open. They were about to hear what the jury had decided. This was the moment Jack had been waiting for, the reason he'd taken the Tony Perez identity, the culmination of his revenge.

A woman stepped into the hall. "He's guilty."

Jack should have felt elation, but all he could do was stare into Caitlyn's blue eyes and hope. "It's over. I'm a free man."

She placed a newspaper in his hand. "The front-page article is about corruption in the U.S. Marshals Service. Patterson and Bryant don't come off well."

They were already in jail, and he hoped they would stay there for a long time. Jack glanced at the article, then back at her. "I guess you made your decision."

"I did." With a manicured fingernail she pointed to the byline. "That's my friend. There's no mention of you or me in the article. I'm just an unnamed source."

"You chose me."

"I chose both," she said. "As a matter of fact, I sold a four-part series to a magazine based on something I learned about when I was with you. Amnesia."

"Is the story about what happened?"

"Not everything is about you, big guy." She grinned. "I've been interviewing shrinks and experts. There's a guy who lost his memory for thirteen years, started a new life and got married. Then he woke up one day and remembered who he was. And a woman who—"

"Little Miss Know-It-All."

"I had to write about it," she said. "Because of you. Because you're unforgettable."

He pulled her into his arms and kissed her. The reality of holding her was better than his memories.

No matter what it took, he would never let her go.

* * * * *

INTRIGUE

COMING NEXT MONTH

Available June 14, 2011

#1281 COWBOY BRIGADE
Daddy Corps
Elle James

#1282 LASSOED
Whitehorse, Montana: Chisholm Cattle Company
B.J. Daniels

#1283 BROKEN
Colby Agency: The New Equalizers
Debra Webb

#1284 THE MISSING TWIN
Guardian Angel Investigations: Lost and Found
Rita Herron

#1285 COOPER VENGEANCE
Cooper Justice: Cold Case Investigation
Paula Graves

#1286 CAPTURING THE COMMANDO
Colleen Thompson

HICNM0511

REQUEST YOUR FREE BOOKS!
2 FREE NOVELS PLUS 2 FREE GIFTS!

Harlequin®

INTRIGUE®

BREATHTAKING ROMANTIC SUSPENSE

YES! Please send me 2 FREE Harlequin Intrigue® novels and my 2 FREE gifts (gifts are worth about $10). After receiving them, if I don't wish to receive any more books, I can return the shipping statement marked "cancel." If I don't cancel, I will receive 6 brand-new novels every month and be billed just $4.24 per book in the U.S. or $4.99 per book in Canada. That's a saving of at least 15% off the cover price! It's quite a bargain! Shipping and handling is just 50¢ per book in the U.S. and 75¢ per book in Canada.* I understand that accepting the 2 free books and gifts places me under no obligation to buy anything. I can always return a shipment and cancel at any time. Even if I never buy another book, the two free books and gifts are mine to keep forever.

182/382 HDN FC5H

Name _____ (PLEASE PRINT)

Address _____ Apt. #

City _____ State/Prov. _____ Zip/Postal Code

Signature (if under 18, a parent or guardian must sign)

Mail to the **Reader Service:**
IN U.S.A.: P.O. Box 1867, Buffalo, NY 14240-1867
IN CANADA: P.O. Box 609, Fort Erie, Ontario L2A 5X3

Not valid for current subscribers to Harlequin Intrigue books.

**Are you a subscriber to Harlequin Intrigue books
and want to receive the larger-print edition?
Call 1-800-873-8635 or visit www.ReaderService.com.**

* Terms and prices subject to change without notice. Prices do not include applicable taxes. Sales tax applicable in N.Y. Canadian residents will be charged applicable taxes. Offer not valid in Quebec. This offer is limited to one order per household. All orders subject to credit approval. Credit or debit balances in a customer's account(s) may be offset by any other outstanding balance owed by or to the customer. Please allow 4 to 6 weeks for delivery. Offer available while quantities last.

Your Privacy—The Reader Service is committed to protecting your privacy. Our Privacy Policy is available online at www.ReaderService.com or upon request from the Reader Service.

We make a portion of our mailing list available to reputable third parties that offer products we believe may interest you. If you prefer that we not exchange your name with third parties, or if you wish to clarify or modify your communication preferences, please visit us at www.ReaderService.com/consumerschoice or write to us at Reader Service Preference Service, P.O. Box 9062, Buffalo, NY 14269. Include your complete name and address.

HI11

Harlequin® Blaze™ brings you
New York Times *and* USA TODAY *bestselling author*
Vicki Lewis Thompson with three new steamy titles
from the bestselling miniseries SONS OF CHANCE

Chance isn't just the last name of these rugged
Wyoming cowboys—it's their motto, too!

Read on for a sneak peek at the first title,
SHOULD'VE BEEN A COWBOY

Available June 2011 only from Harlequin® Blaze™.

"THANKS FOR NOT TURNING ON THE LIGHTS," Tyler said. "I'm a mess."

"Not in my book." Even in low light, Alex had a good view of her yellow shirt plastered to her body. It was all he could do not to reach for her, mud and all. But the next move needed to be hers, not his.

She slicked her wet hair back and squeezed some water out of the ends as she glanced upward. "I like the sound of the rain on a tin roof."

"Me, too."

She met his gaze briefly and looked away. "Where's the sink?"

"At the far end, beyond the last stall."

Tyler's running shoes squished as she walked down the aisle between the rows of stalls. She glanced sideways at Alex. "So how much of a cowboy are you these days? Do you ride the range and stuff?"

"I ride." He liked being able to say that. "Why?"

"Just wondered. Last summer, you were still a city boy. You even told me you weren't the cowboy type, but you're…different now."

He wasn't sure if that was a good thing or a bad thing. Maybe she preferred city boys to cowboys. "How am I different?"

"Well, you dress differently, and your hair's a little longer. Your face seems a little more chiseled, but maybe that's because of your hair. Also, there's something else, something harder to define, an attitude…"

"Are you saying I have an attitude?"

"Not in a bad way. It's more like a quiet confidence."

He was flattered, but still he had to laugh. "I just admitted a while ago that I have all kinds of doubts about this event tomorrow. That doesn't seem like quiet confidence to me."

"This isn't about your job, it's about…your…" She took a deep breath. "It's about your sex appeal, okay? I have no business talking about it, because it will only make me want to do things I shouldn't do." She started toward the end of the barn. "Now, where's that sink? We need to get cleaned up and go back to the house. Dinner is probably ready, and I—"

He spun her around and pulled her into his arms, mud and all. "Let's do those things." Then he kissed her, knowing that she would kiss him back, knowing that this time he would take that kiss where he wanted it to go. And she would let him.

Follow Tyler and Alex's wild adventures in
SHOULD'VE BEEN A COWBOY
Available June 2011 only from Harlequin® Blaze™
wherever books are sold.

INTRIGUE®

USA TODAY BESTSELLING AUTHOR

B.J. DANIELS

**BRINGS READERS THE NEXT
INSTALLMENT IN THE SUSPENSEFUL
MINISERIES**

WHITEHORSE
MONTANA

Chisholm Cattle Company

When Billie Rae Rasmussen literally crashes into
handsome rancher Tanner Chisholm at the local rodeo,
the explosion is bigger than the fair's fireworks.

Tanner quickly realizes this frightened woman
is running from a dark and dangerous secret.

Can he save her?

LASSOED
June 2011

Four more titles to follow....

HI69549

SPECIAL EDITION

Life, Love and Family

LOVE CAN BE FOUND IN THE MOST UNLIKELY PLACES, ESPECIALLY WHEN YOU'RE NOT LOOKING FOR IT...

Failed marriages, broken families and disappointment. Cecilia and Brandon have both been unlucky in love and life and are ripe for an intervention. Good thing Brandon's mother happens to stumble upon this matchmaking project. But will Brandon be able to open his eyes and get away from his busy career to see that all he needs is right there in front of him?

FIND OUT IN

WHAT THE SINGLE DAD WANTS...

BY *USA TODAY* BESTSELLING AUTHOR

MARIE FERRARELLA

AVAILABLE IN JUNE 2011
WHEREVER BOOKS ARE SOLD.